# The Infinite Jeff
## A Parable of Change

### — Part 1 —
### Journey into Insight

Second Edition

## BY
## Will Holcomb

will@willholcombauthor.com

# ₂Havens
## PUBLISHING

ISBN 978-0-9916311-3-1
Updated: 07/26/2021
Amazon Version

Cover design Marina Petric & Jose Gomez

# Dedication

To my wife, Lisa, for putting up with me while writing this in the precious spare time which could have been used to clean the garage. And to my sister, Jackie, through her patience and guidance, turned me into a writer.

– Part 1 –

# Blog Post #1
# Stanley Whitmore

"The mass of men lead lives of quiet desperation." Henry David Thoreau's words have rung true in my head since the first time I read them in *Walden*. As I watch people at work, in the grocery store, and even in the park with their kids, I can see Thoreau's quiet desperation etched in their faces. It seems even after all these years, the mass of men is *still* struggling to find their way to happiness and meaning. And I am just one of the mass searching for meaning.

Church and religion have a long history of bringing meaning to people's lives, but as hard as I try, meaning from that source is evasive. I still go, for family consistency, but as I look around at the others who sit with me in Sunday services, it seems so easy for them to accept what's being said as absolute truth. I envy them. Faith is a fleeting concept to me. I listen and try to believe, but can't.

The church's minister is a great person, one of the few people I know who genuinely seems to have taken his religion's message of love to heart. The rest of his message, I either don't get or think is simply wrong. For him, I can overlook the discrepancy and be glad he believes what he believes because his beliefs make him a truly *good* person. Regrettably, I can't seem to overlook the church's assumption science and religion are mutually exclusive.

Another logical place to look for meaning is in my work. When I was young and idealistic, I dreamed of being a high school English teacher. But after graduation, my idealism quickly soured as I faced the reality of a classroom that was more about test scores than learning. On the rebound, I took a job as a technical writer, which was only supposed to pay the bills until I found a *real* job, but after that, the only doors which seemed to open were tech-writing doors. In some ways, it's good, because I love technology, but lately, the only meaning I've found in my job comes every other Friday, hopefully before my checking account's balance goes negative.

The next logical place to look for meaning is with my family. And my family *is* the one place in my life where meaning rings true, even in the worst of times. If I had to give an example of one thing I do right, it would be: being a great dad to my kids. Being a great husband needs more work; it seems cleaning the garage, helping with laundry, buying flowers, and curbing a highly refined sense of humor are all skills I need to work on. My wife puts up with me with remarkable equanimity. She is a much better wife than I am a husband and a spectacular mom. When I get off the treadmill-of-life long enough to stop taking them for granted, I know I am truly blessed with my wife and kids.

But, while vitally important to me, finding meaning only within the arms of my family isn't enough.

As I move forward through my life, putting one foot awkwardly in front of the other, Mr. Thoreau's words continue to ring in my head, and I wonder: Am I wrong to crave more out of life than quiet desperation? Am I wrong to yearn for meaning? Or does life have no meaning?

When I look up at the sky, some days I *know* there *is* something guiding the Universe. Other days, I sit in church trying to believe, wishing I could. But most of the time when I look up, I feel this life is a great cosmic fluke, and I'm only a chemical reaction trying to assign reason where none exists.

# -- Part 1 --

# Chapter 1

*Bakersfield, California*
*Sunday evening, early July*

"Stanley Whitmore," my wife, Beth, said in amused reproach as she loaded the dishwasher with the Sunday dinner plates our eight-year-old son, Cooper, handed her, "life is more than a cosmic fluke and getting laid off five months ago was not a cosmic sucker punch." She shook her head in mock resignation. I'm sure she was wondering why she said 'yes' eleven years ago.

Assuming she wasn't too impressed with my first attempt at blogging, in return, I fought my never-ending battle of trying to put my thoughts into words which made sense to her. "Sure it is." I handed her the scraped serving dishes. "I now have absolute proof the Universe revolves around me. Proof its whole purpose is to keep me stressed out." I leaned against the kitchen counter, arms crossed, waiting for her rebuttal.

She smiled at me with a face that made me glad I worked up the nerve eleven years ago to ask her. "Poor Stanley. You lost a job you hated, haven't been able to find one as quick as you wanted, and now this is all part of some master universal conspiracy against you." She shared a grin with our six-year-old daughter, Alice--named after my mother, but the spitting image of Beth with the same wavy brown hair.

I quickly raised my hand, pointed at Beth, and triumphantly exclaimed, "Exactly! Now you're seeing it!" Beth's ability to joke with me and support me during the last five months had saved me from a nervous breakdown or worse.

I shared a smile with Cooper as he carried the last of the dirty dishes to Beth. Every day he looked more like Beth's father--who he was named after--and I couldn't wish a better future for the kid. I winked at him, and he grinned back.

"Daddy?"

I glanced over at Alice to let her know she had my attention. She stood there, her small arms loaded with the day's recycling to take out to the bin. One good thing about having to stop all our extracurricular activities due to lack of money was that we ate dinner together almost every night and had the clean-up system down to a science. Cooper liked taking the food scraps out to the compost pile because he got to dig in the dirt.

"Was Mr. Allen part of the comic flute that made you sad?"

I smiled to myself at her misspoken 'comic flute,' then her words sunk in and I sobered at the gravity of her question. I looked at Beth for support, but her shrug put it all back on me. Dan Allen-- the much-loved minister of the church Beth grew up in--had dropped dead from a heart attack at a church softball game a few weeks ago. The church was in deep mourning, so were my family and I. "No, Alice, that cosmic fluke--" and it truly was; he was a beautiful man, and the church was lost without his example "-- makes more than me sad. I think you could tell that at church this morning."

Alice nodded in wide-eyed agreement. "I wanted him there today. The man who preached scared me." Then she left to take the recycling out.

I understood all too well what she was feeling. Dan wasn't a 'feel good' preacher, one who made me feel warm and fuzzy, yet his message usually pushed my limits in a direction that made me want to learn to love even half as well as he loved every day of his life. His last sermon before he died was on Jesus' parable of the Good Samaritan. I left church that Sunday ready to find a neighbor to love.

That sermon was a stark difference from today's sermon from the man auditioning to fill Dan's shoes. I left church this morning feeling dirty, defiled, and angry; this man's message was condemning and hateful. His 'us vs. them' message, laced with military metaphors such as 'we're in a battle' and 'we can't let the enemy win,' found no home in my heart.

Beth was almost sick as we drove home, feeling the church she grew up in was gone. She was used to Mr. Allen (she had never gotten past her childhood formality), who almost every Sunday would belt out his off-key version of the old spiritual *Down by the Riverside* with the refrain, "Ain't gonna study war no more."

Outside Dan's theology of love, he and I had little in common on the subject of religion. He, along with most of the church members, subscribed to what is known as 'Young Earth Creationism' and other associated dogma, which I felt was an unhealthy interpretation of the Bible. I grew up in a different brand of Christianity, and after eleven years of going to Beth's church, listening to people with little or no knowledge of biology, geology, paleontology, or any other 'ologies, proclaim with certainty (based on a few out-of-context verses from the Bible) the Earth was less than ten thousand years old and evolution was a conspiracy to turn everyone into atheists, my confidence in anything they had to say was almost nonexistent. As a result, I felt like my already weak Christian faith was being extinguished. But Dan had been a heck of a great guy. I loved him to death.

As Alice had unintentionally changed the mood, we finished cleaning up without much being said.

After that, I headed to the living room to watch TV, then stopped and laughed at my habit. The cable was a victim of my unemployment. I didn't mind the cable being shut off, except for my severe Sci-Fi channel withdrawal. Cutting the phone off had been a relief because the bill collectors didn't have our cell phone numbers. And we'd sold the car with the most equity and bought a cheap one with the left-over cash.

Without the TV option, we grabbed a board game and finished the night by reading to the kids before bed.

In many ways, like the amount of time we spent with the kids, we were coming out ahead with me being laid off. But we'd had to remove the kids from all their after-school stuff--dance, karate, and scouts--and I hated that. We'd also dropped our gym membership, which had been tough on Beth; she enjoyed her exercise classes. Racquetball was the only thing I used the gym for. I'd played racquetball since college and enjoyed it, so it was hard to give that up.

We had to quit giving at the church, other than the token dollar to set an example for the kids, and that was hard. Even though I'm technically not a member of the church and disagree with them on many theological grounds, I agreed with them in areas far more important. They have outreach programs such as a food pantry, a local children's home, a nursing home, and several other programs which help people in need.

In fact, the latter may soon include us. They have repeatedly offered to help us with utility bills and food, and I felt humbled by their generosity. So far, we hadn't gotten to the point where we have had to accept, but it's getting close.

Beth's income from her portrait painting business typically made enough to help, but business was down due to the economy. She'd thought about getting a different job. With an art degree and no work experience at anything other than painting, she hadn't found work which contributed much more than she was already making, so we decided at least one of us should be able to do what they loved. Besides, I loved seeing her paint. It's a talent I truly appreciated, mildly envied, and wouldn't do anything to hurt.

As I spent the rest of the evening fruitlessly searching the web for jobs, worry was my companion, and I watched Beth's mood sink further.

\* \* \*

As we were getting ready for bed that night, I could tell Beth was deep in thought. Still mired in job-search-hazed thoughts, I wasn't in a mood to talk, so I hoped I could get to bed and asleep before she felt the need to confide in me. But my desire for marital harmony overcame my frustrations, and I finally realized I was being a jerk; the Universe was about more than me, and I should think about someone else.

Of course, the best time to ask was when she's brushing her teeth. Okay, the brushing teeth thing was poor planning, which became obvious from the look she gave me when I asked her what she was thinking seconds after she put the toothbrush in her mouth.

Beth finished brushing, hung her toothbrush in the holder, leaned with locked arms on the counter, and looked at our reflections in the mirror.

As she formed her response, I walked over to stand beside her and studied her reflection. Her brown hair was pulled back in a ponytail so she could wash the make-up off her face. I'd known her for five years before we were married, and she was more beautiful now than when we met. I looked at my reflection and couldn't say the same. We were both thirty-nine, but only I looked it.

Her eyes locked on mine in the mirror and she began. "I was thinking..."

Immediately, the usual question popped in my head when I hear her say those words, "How much will it cost?" and I guess the usual expression appeared on my face because she answered it.

"It won't cost anything. Well, I mean it will cost something but not really."

I looked at my likeness in the mirror, examining my puzzled face, but said nothing. Her image looked like it was going to continue without my input.

"I haven't been able to stop thinking since church." Our eyes met in the mirror. "I've lost my church home." I saw them start to water. "I know you go there for me and the kids. And, for me, this church was why I have wanted to stay in Bakersfield." The water in one of her eyes was starting to form a tear. "But you can't seem to get a job around here and Bakersfield isn't overflowing with tech companies."

I couldn't believe what I was hearing; I'd long ago reconciled myself to never moving because of her connections to her childhood home and its community roots. Turning to face her, I asked, "You can't be serious, Beth? What about your parents?"

"They'll understand." She swiped the tear away. "How can they not understand? You have to have a job. Our credit cards are about maxed out, and we aren't going to have the money to pay the mortgage next month. We have to do something."

"This is big, Beth. I never thought you would say something like this." I placed my hand on her back and rubbed gently.

She looked down into the sink. "Everything seems to be pointing to that. I don't think we have another choice."

She was right, but I wasn't going to say that, so I offered her some time. "Let's talk about it in the morning."

She looked at my duplicate in the mirror again, and I focused on hers. With another tear slowly making its way past her nose, she tried to smile and with no sound mouthed, "Okay."

We went to bed and I fell into an uneasy sleep. Beth giving up Bakersfield was something I never thought would happen. She was more upset about the church service than I'd realized.

I dozed on and off, but by four in the morning I gave up.

Quietly, I got out of bed, headed through the dark house to the study, and turned on the computer.

As it booted up, I idly twisted in my desk chair and tried to understand what moving would mean to Beth. This was where she grew up. Her parents still lived here. She had a huge circle of friends here, and normally a thriving business. Her church was a big part of her life.

As for me, I'd moved here because of her. Her parents were very cool, but no reason for me to stay, and her church drove me nuts. I missed the relative sanity of the church I'd grown up in and it would be nice to live closer to my parents in Washington. We don't get to see them as much as I would like. Seattle is much more abundant for my line of work.

Once the computer was up, I went to the main job site I'd been using and pulled up my profile.

The box entitled 'Willing to relocate' was unchecked. I placed the mouse cursor over it, ready to click, then took my hand off the mouse and leaned back in the chair, looking at the checkbox.

I'd told Beth we would talk about it in the morning. It was her decision, not mine. I'd leave this place in a heartbeat, so moving wasn't for me to come to terms with.

Then I thought, if I did check the box and, if by some small chance, I got a call but Beth had changed her mind, I could say 'no' and uncheck it as easily as I checked it.

I reached out, pressed the mouse button to check the box, and quickly clicked 'save' before I changed my mind.

It felt like the right thing to do, and it was so simple two clicks. But man! It somehow felt like it changed everything.

Then I pulled up my new blog to see if anyone had viewed it. It still wasn't clear in my mind why I was even experimenting with blogging. I wasn't sure what I'd hoped to accomplish but it wouldn't hurt to try, and maybe, I'd see some benefit. It showed one view already. I guess that was a start.

Needing to work off some nervous energy, I wandered out to the backyard, closing the sliding door softly behind me. It was a beautiful night with the temperature just right.

I wandered to the pool and stood on the first step staring down into the water and wondered if, after eleven years in this house, eleven years of standing in this pool, if sometime in the near future I'd never be able to do this again.

Then I walked over to my feeble attempt at a compost pile, grabbed the nearby shovel, and gave the pile a turn. Beth and I have never had much success with vegetable gardening, but we had fun trying. Looking across the yard at the dead plants in our garden, I wondered if I'd get to test the compost on it.

It was strange to think about leaving. It was hard to wrap my mind around it.

After about twenty minutes of drifting thoughts but no reduction in anxiety, I figured I might as well go back to bed where I might not sleep, but at least I wouldn't get stickers in my bare feet.

\* \* \*

Morning came. When I was working, I'd hated Mondays, and now that I'd been unemployed for so long, I still hated them. I didn't feel like getting up, but I didn't feel like lying there either. A no-win situation. But I guess I must have slept some because Beth was gone and I hadn't noticed.

With a gargantuan effort, I heaved myself out of bed, slipped on a pair of shorts, and headed to the kitchen, where Beth was reading. The kids were still asleep.

She looked over the top of her book and gave me a playful, horrified face. "Rough night?"

I lumbered to the fridge, found a half-full can of Mt. Dew, and then plunked into a chair at the table with her. "No. Slept like a baby."

She set her book on the table and nodded in an understanding way. "I see. A baby who wanders around the backyard at five in the morning?"

"Yeah, that kind of baby."

She looked out the kitchen window into the backyard for a few minutes before softly voicing her thoughts. "I might've been too hasty last night. I was upset about church. I'm sure better ministers will be applying. There's no way they'll hire the guy yesterday. Mr. Allen will be hard to replace, but maybe they'll get someone good."

Instantly regretting last night's action, I clenched my hands around the cold can. "I guess I was too hasty, too," I reluctantly admitted. "I updated my job site profile with 'Willing to relocate.'" I began to stand. "I'll go uncheck it right now. Sorry. Should've waited until we talked."

She smiled gently at me and waved me back into the chair. "That anxious to leave?" She took a drink from her glass. "Leave it checked for now. I can't imagine having a check in a box will magically change anything; you haven't heard anything from anybody in weeks."

I took a long drink from my Dew to finish it off and wondered how long it had been in the fridge; it was flat. It really doesn't hit the spot when it's like that.

As I got up, hoping to find an unopened can in the fridge, I realized how relieved I was to hear her say to leave the box checked. I didn't mess up too badly then. I gave her a grateful smile and said "Okay" as I searched the fridge for a cold Dew.

Suddenly, my cell phone rang in my bedroom, loud enough I feared it would wake the kids, so I closed the fridge and quietly rushed down the hall. As usual, I was too late.

I didn't recognize the number, so I stuck the phone in my shorts pockets, went back to the fridge, and joyfully found my much-needed drink behind the salad dressing. I popped the top and headed back to the table.

Beth was looking out the window again and without turning, she said, "On second thought. Uncheck it for now. I'm not ready yet." Life isn't so bad, I thought philosophically. The non-flat Dew hit the spot, and I wasn't in trouble for checking the box without talking to her. While looking out the window, she must have seen the freshly turned compost pile and had a change of heart. I didn't blame her; I'd finally figured this compost-thing out and it'd definitely make the difference in the garden next year. "I'll do it right now." And headed to the study.

At the computer, I pulled up my email and a browser. Quickly glancing at the email subjects, my heart jumped at a subject line I had seen only a handful of times in the last five months: 'About your resume.'

I dreaded opening it. Up until now, such emails had only given me false hope and ultimately, disappointment. With great reservation, I double-clicked on the email header:

*Hi Stanley,*

*This is Tom from Havens Research Institute. I just left you a phone message. Sorry to call you so early but please give me a call back as soon as you can. After looking at your resume, I think we have a great opportunity for you. Sorry to seem impatient but we need to fill this quickly and I wanted to get to you before someone else did.*

*Looking forward to hearing from you,*

*Tom*

"Beth!" I yelled as I copied and pasted the company name into the browser's search box, and then winced when I remembered the kids were still asleep. But that worry was quickly forgotten as I re-read the email. Its tone was different from the rest. In my mind, it didn't read as a polite inquiry, but instead, it read as a strong possibility.

When Beth hurried into the room, I pointed at the email.

She leaned on my chair and over my shoulder, read the email. "Where are they?"

I clicked on the first link from the search results and we watched the page load. Once it was done, I scanned the page for the quickest way to answer her question. One click on 'Contact Us' and we had the answer: Bethlehem, Pennsylvania. The other side of America.

I listened for her reaction.

"That was fast," she said slowly, obviously thinking through her words before she said them. "I mean, you clicked that box at four this morning and got a hit already. Maybe you should've checked that box a few months ago if it's this easy."

Beth's words were music to my ears. With the highly emotional attachment she had to this area, I'd expected the opposite. I looked at her trying to hide my surprise. "You're okay with this?"

She shrugged. "I don't see we have much choice. You at least need to check it out." I nodded in agreement and she continued, "Maybe it's fate. Maybe this is the way it's meant to happen."

"Sure, Beth. Some divine entity wants me to uproot my family and go work as a tech writer in Pennsylvania."

I was partly joking and partly not; I'd grown impatient with that kind of talk at her church. A couple of Sundays ago, one of the members had stood in front of the church and thanked them for their prayers after she'd cut her toe off with a garden shovel. She said she didn't always understand God's will but was trying to learn from the experience. Sure, I'd said to myself as I sat in the pew staring in disbelief like maybe you should learn not to wear flip-flops when using a shovel. Anyone would be hard pressed to convince me God had anything to do with it.

As for fate stepping in to send me a job email, I don't think their God--who was so busy condemning people to eternal damnation because they were unfortunate enough to be born into the wrong belief system--was all that concerned about my job any more than He was involved with the lady's gardening stupidity.

However, I'll bet He's impressed with my compost pile.

Of course, I didn't say any of that to Beth. Over the years, I'd learned that never goes well.

And I was saved from the temptation when a stray neuron struck and I remembered the phone call I'd missed. I picked up my cell phone and saw there was a voicemail.

I looked over my shoulder and met Beth's gaze, then turned back and dialed, putting it on the speaker so Beth could hear, too.

Tom's voice came from the little machine, giving me the same impression as the email, this wasn't one in an endless list of impersonal calls the guy was making.

After I turned off the phone, Beth gave me an impatient nudge. "Well? Call him back."

I glanced at the clock; it was only seven.

"Stanley, he just called you, so he must be in his office. Besides, on the East coast, it's well into their workday."

After taking a deep breath, I bowed to her logic, picked up the phone, and redialed the call. As it connected, the butterflies started fluttering in my gut, and I wished I'd taken a few minutes to research more about the company.

The same voice answered, "Hello, this is Tom."

Trying to relax and not walk all over my words, as calmly as I could, I said, "Hi, Tom. This is Stanley Whitmore."

"Stanley! Glad you called back so quickly. I was checking the job website this morning and your resume came up. It looked right for a tech writing position here at Havens Research Institute. Are you still available?"

Another deep breath and a comforting pat from Beth. "Yes, I am."

"That's great. You got a minute for a quick rundown of the contract?"

I tried not to sigh into the phone. I'd hoped for a permanent job but, financially, I was past the beggars-couldn't-be-choosers stage.

Unaware of my trepidation, Tom kept right on. "We're an R&D center, and one of our projects is screaming at me to get a good tech writer for the end of the project. This is a two-month contract. Is that okay?"

I didn't know how to answer that and paused a second before saying, "Well, I..."

He must have heard my hesitation, so didn't give me time to continue. "Stanley, listen. I'm sure you'd rather have a permanent gig but we really need this filled and we need it soon. Here's what it's worth to me." He gave me the hourly rate, and I about dropped the phone.

I wrote it on a piece of paper and showed Beth who was

hovering over me. Her eyes lit up.

"Does that help with the reservations you have?" Tom asked.

Beth pushed me out of the way of the desk drawer and dug out the calculator.

Not sure if I should feel better or more nervous because this was now high stakes, I answered truthfully, "Yes. That helps."

He continued, "Good. And while you're out here you'll be on per diem so that should help also."

Trying not to sound too excited, I replied, "That works for me."

"Good. Listen, Stanley, I'm not going to ask a bunch of technical stuff because I'd be lying if I said I understood the project. So, I want to set up a phone interview with the manager. This afternoon, if possible. He can ask you all that technical stuff. But if you're half as good as your resume looks, you'll be fine."

My thought was: 'you mean the resume everybody has ignored for five months?' But instead, I replied, "Sure, I can do that."

"Great! Two o'clock your time okay?"

"That sounds great."

Tom ended the call with, "Expect a call at two and I look forward to meeting you."

# Chapter 2

After I pressed 'end call,' I looked up at Beth who was eagerly waiting to hear the other half of the conversation. The hourly rate had me nervous. I only said, "Wow!"

She asked, "Other than the pay, how's it sound?"

"I'd be gone for two months, but the money would mean we could stay here and I'd have more time to try and find a job in *this* area."

Beth and I looked at each other for a moment. I knew she wasn't happy about the idea of me working across the country, but she was even less enthusiastic about having the house foreclosed on. She shrugged. "Looks like we've got some research to do before two."

I nodded, turned back to my computer, she went to hers, and that's how we spent the next hour.

Bethlehem, Pennsylvania was about twenty-seven hundred miles away. We read more on Havens Research Institute and as much as we wanted to, we couldn't think of a reason not to take the contract if I could get it.

After we ate breakfast with the kids, we shooed them outside and Beth and I sat down again in the study.

"It sounds like a good place, Stanley. Sounds like a place you'd like."

"I don't know," I replied, staring out the window at the kids playing on the swing set. "I'd hoped for a chance at something new, something more, not another tech writer job. They're all the same."

"Stanley." She looked at me intently. "That's what you applied for."

It's hard to argue with logic like that.

She gave me an endearing grin not saying anything else about my lack of logic. "Maybe after you come back from this because of course, you're going to get it, then what about going back into the occupation you actually went to school for? You know, use your degree."

After my student teaching experience, my idealistic thoughts of inspiring kids to love literature, like a teacher had done for me, were extinguished. I hated being hogtied by all the state's and school's guidelines. Because of all the rules, I couldn't make the class interesting enough to inspire anyone. I was even more in awe of my Lit teacher after that; I couldn't do what she had done and I wasn't going to pretend I could. "No. Failing at that once was enough."

I stood, went to the window, leaned against the frame, absently watching Alice chase her brother after he'd nabbed her jump rope-- the kid was asking for trouble if his sister caught him; she wasn't a shrinking violet--and reflected on my job prospects some more.

I didn't seem to fit anywhere. It wasn't even an issue of a square peg in a round hole. It was like I was some amorphous-shaped peg and I didn't even know where the stupid hole was.

"What shape am I?" I asked Beth, turning to her, and when she looked at me like I'd lost my mind, I clarified. "I'm not teacher-shaped and never really been tech writer shaped, even if I can pretend I am. How come I've never been able to figure out what shape of a hole I fit into?"

"Maybe it'll be different this time," she said, trying to be encouraging. She crossed the room to stand in front of me. "And if not, it's only two months. After that, we'll have some money set aside and maybe you can take some time to try to figure out what shape you are." She patted my middle-aged stomach and teased, "Personally, I like your 'Stanley' shape."

I smiled. That was pretty funny. "You're right. I can make it for two months--if I can even get the job. But if I do get it and if we're careful, we should be able to save enough to get us by for a while."

I spent the rest of the morning alternating between trying to prepare for the interview and trying to distract myself from it. I surfed the web, checked my blog stats, which still showed only one view, and read more about HRI.

Cooper helped add to my distraction by sitting in the study with me, at Beth's computer, and watching YouTube music videos. He's only allowed to watch them when Beth or I are around. This did two things for me, it exercised my self-control to not yell, 'Turn that *noise* off!' and gave me more respect for my parents putting up with my music. So, I cruised HRI's website while rap music played in the background. At least the guy Cooper had been listening to lately wasn't as annoying as some.

"Hey, Dad, what's the name of this video?"

I needed to get out of the chair anyway, so I walked over to look at his screen. "Nineveh."

"What's that mean?"

I shrugged. "Sounds familiar but I don't remember." I went back to my desk as he clicked the play button and was pleasantly surprised to hear a guitar instrumental start, so I sat and listened for a minute.

Technically, it was an outstanding piece of work. As an unaccomplished guitarist myself, I appreciated the intricacies of the song, which seemed to draw you in and keep you hooked. "Keep listening to him, Cooper. I like this guy."

My kid was focused on the computer and didn't turn to me when he answered with dripping sarcasm, "That's 'The Change,' Dad. The same guy I've been listening to for the last half hour."

"He's actually pretty good. Maybe if I get this job, I can start up my guitar lessons again and be as good as he is in a couple years."

Cooper gave a disparaging snort. "Get real, Dad."

I chuckled. I had been taking lessons for a bunch of years, and even with consistent practice, I'm by no means good. I occasionally wondered if I was attempting to do something my brain wasn't wired for. Yet, in a strange way, that's what I like about it; it felt like I was working a part of my brain which needed the workout.

And thinking about guitars and my brain was more interesting than thinking about my upcoming interview.

\* \* \*

By 1:30, my nerves were shot. At 1:50, I kicked Cooper out and made death threats to the kids for them to stay quiet or get out of the house. As the clock on my computer changed to 2:00, my phone rang.

I took a deep breath, let the phone ring once more before picking it up. "Hello, this is Stanley."

"Hello, Stanley. This is Aaron with Havens Research Institute. We have an interview set up for two o'clock. You ready?"

"Yes. Now's a great time."

"Wonderful. How's the weather in California?"

So far so good. I knew the answer to this question, but I looked out the window to make sure. "It's sunny and hot, but that's a normal day here."

"Wonderful. You ready for a change of weather?"

"Sure, I could use some cooler weather."

"Wonderful. I bet you could. When can you start?"

"My schedule's open right now." I was confused as to why Aaron asked that question so early in the interview.

"Wonderful. Would you be able to start in a week? Next Monday?"

I paused. Was I misunderstanding him? "Sure, that would work out good for me."

"Wonderful! See you then. Actually, I'll see you Tuesday. They'll have you doing the normal HR, finance, and meet the CEO stuff on Monday."

He'd paused as if waiting for an answer, but I was still waiting for the technical questions to start, so I was mightily confused and didn't know what to say. "Okay," I said with some uncertainty.

"It was great talking to you, and I look forward to meeting you in person next Tuesday."

Totally dumbfounded, I replied, "I look forward to meeting you, too."

"Wonderful. You'll be getting some emails here shortly. Bye"

"Bye," I answered, but the phone was already dead on the other end.

I stared at my phone for a long minute, wondering what had happened, then walked out of the study to my anxious wife. She looked at the clock. It read 2:03, and as she looked at it, it changed to 2:04. She got a worried look on her face.

"I start next Monday," I stated, still roiling in confusion.

She smiled in relief. "Thank you, God! That's great. It was pretty short. What'd he ask you?"

"He asked me how the weather was here." I thought about that for a second. "That's it. I spent all day reading, preparing, worrying, and he asked me how the weather was. Oh, he also asked if I was ready for a change in weather."

She tried to smile a reassuring smile, but her confusion almost equaled mine. "Well, I guess you must have done a great job answering that."

"Must have. But did you hear me? Monday. A week from today. Twenty-seven-hundred miles." We'd already briefly talked logistics as we'd researched and flying would cost three times as much as driving thanks to a forty-five MPG car. So, I'd be driving cross-country. I quickly counted days. "I'd have to leave Wednesday morning. That leaves one whole day to arrange everything."

Beth let that thought settle for a moment, then said in her best practical voice, "We'd best get cracking!"

So we did.

\* \* \*

"Are you listening to me, Stanley?" Beth called from the open garage doorway early Wednesday morning.

I looked back over my shoulder at her. Cooper and I were precariously leaned into the back of my blue Jetta wagon--royal blue, Beth told me repeatedly--trying to wrestle a duffle into a space far too small. "Now I am."

Beth continued in the same tone, "Did you get the first aid kit out of the bathroom? The one I reminded you three times about?"

I did a quick mental search of all the things I'd so far squeezed into the car in the hour since breakfast and didn't come up with a first aid kit. "Apparently not."

She gave an exasperated sigh and jerked her thumb at Alice, who ran into the house to fetch the box. Then Beth placed her hands on her hips--very nice hips I'd always thought--and ordered, "Cooper go into the house and get the small cooler from the kitchen. And, Stanley, what else did you forget?"

As the kid left, I considered how one goes about answering that question without getting into trouble. I discarded several smart-aleck remarks, knowing my "refined" sense of humor wasn't appreciated by my spouse to the extent I thought it should be, and finally said, "If I remembered, would they be forgotten?"

Throwing up her hands, she turned back into the house, so I went back to contemplating the duffel bag. I'd hoped to leave the back passenger seat empty so I could fully recline the front passenger seat, in hopes of getting a decent night's sleep. Paying the mortgage came before my comfort, so hotels were a luxury I'd have to forego; paying for the gas would be hard enough. Thank goodness, the Jetta was a diesel with great gas mileage or we'd have been in an even bigger mess than we were. My 'save the world' mentality was going to save me a butt-load of money on this trip.

Besides, this wouldn't be the first time I'd done a cross-country trip living out of my car, sustained by a cooler full of sandwiches and Mountain Dew--the nectar of the gods. Granted, the last time I'd done it was almost twenty years ago, but hey, I'm only thirty-nine now, not that old, I could do it again.

"Here, Dad," Alice announced from behind me.

I turned as she extended the white plastic box. Spying my wife again standing by the door, I leaned down to my daughter as I took the box and spoke loud enough I knew Beth could hear. "Thanks, Thing 2, and this is an important thing for you to remember when you get married. Nothing says, 'I love you' like a well-packed first aid kit."

"Da-a-a-d," Alice replied in the tone that only she could manage, making the word at least four syllables long instead of its normal one.

I chuckled and ruffled her hair. As she leaned into my leg, I tucked the white box into the spot I'd been trying to stuff the duffel bag into, and tossed the duffel into the backseat. When I stopped for the night, I could always shove the bag on top of the rest of the stuff, then in the morning move it back into the seat so I had a clear view out the rear window.

"Dad!" Cooper called. "Open the door."

I nudged Alice, and she scooted around the car and opened the driver's side back door for her brother, who was lugging a small cooler, big for an eight-year-old, down the sun-dappled driveway.

"You got it, Coop?" I asked, but let him manfully struggle with the burden almost too big for him.

"Of course," he grunted, and managed to heave the cooler onto the backseat beside the big cooler I'd brought out earlier.

"Good. I think that's it," I announced, then glanced at Beth. "Anything left in the house?"

"That's it as far as I know," she answered.

"Cool!" I closed the wagon's hatch with a final-sounding thunk.

As I turned to face the house, Alice came and leaned against my leg again, and Cooper stopped a couple of steps behind her, trying for manly stoicism. But I could see the tears behind his determination to be strong, and it hurt. I'd gone on the odd business trip or two, but I'd never been away from them for more than a couple of days, and the thought of being away from them and Beth had tears welling behind my eyes. However, having a few more years of practice than my son, I put on a smile and squatted down so I was eye-level with Alice.

"Can I send you back something when I get there? Maybe a T-shirt that says 'Thing 2'--" I raised my hands then drew them apart the width of her body "--in really big letters. And--" I forced a grin, inviting her to share the family joke over their constant bickering as to who did more work around the house "--I'll get one for Cooper that says 'Thing 1' in really little letters?"

As Alice smiled, Cooper heaved an exasperated sigh. Before her brother could get a word in Alice spoke up, "What I want is a big-people T-shirt that says Havers... Haverst Research..."

"Havens Research Institute," I supplied.

"Yeah, that, across the front in big letters. I can sleep in it at night and pretend you're here and hugging me instead of so far away."

"Aw, Alice," I murmured as I pulled her into a hug, and had to blink tears away as I looked to Beth and saw her swipe her cheeks. "This sucks," I mouthed to my wife, so my kids wouldn't hear. She shrugged and gave me a we-gotta-do-what-we-gotta-do look. Had to pay the bills, end of story.

Taking a deep breath to get my expression back under control, I tucked Alice to my side, twisted slightly to face Cooper, and pulled him to my empty side. "What can I get you, Thing 1? Do you want a Havens shirt, too?"

He leaned his arm across my shoulder as I tightened my grip on his waist. "No, I want a shirt from 'The Change.'"

Confused, I looked at him. "What?"

"You know. The rapper you liked."

Now I was more confused. Me liking a rapper made no sense.

Cooper gave another exasperated look and tried to remind me. "He had the guitar song with the funny name you liked."

"Oh, that one. Granted, it's an impressive song, but don't go telling people I like rap music."

He grinned at me, crossing his heart.

"How am I supposed to get you a shirt from him?"

"He lives out in Pennsylvania somewhere."

Not sure how to respond I gave a non-committal shrug. "Okay. If I happen to run into 'The Change,' I'll see if he'll give me a T-shirt for you."

I hugged them hard enough they both squealed, then I followed a tradition we called 'Seussing.' I'm not sure when we started doing it, but we all liked trying to make up Dr. Seuss types of rhymes. That is where the nicknames 'Thing 1' and 'Thing 2' got cast upon my poor kids.

> *"Tho I may be leaving,*
> *Driving into the sun,*
> *Wondering if I can smile*
> *Without my little Thing 1.*
> *And way 'cross the country,*
> *I'll try not to be blue,*
> *'Cause I don't know if I can make it*
> *Without my little Thing 2."*

They both forced a smile and hugged me tighter. Cooper let a tear flow and tried to hide it.

I pretended not to notice and with a laugh, I let them go, stood, and stepped to their mother. "I'm sorry I have to leave you alone." I cupped her cheek with my hand. "Your folks are on the other side of town, so you'll have them nearby if you need anything."

"I know," Beth replied as she hugged me. "I'll be okay. It's only for a couple months. And if we keep to our budget, this'll be enough money to last for several months after you get back, surely long enough to find another job." She leaned back and gave me a watery smile. "And maybe they'll like you enough they'll hire you full-time, and we'll all move out there to be with you."

"We can only hope." After I said that, the realization of the statement's implications actually hit me kind of hard. Once we'd opened up the prospect of leaving our 'home,' it seemed like it wasn't quite 'our home' anymore.

"Hey," she said, as she gave her cheeks another quick swipe before the kids noticed. "Maybe you can check out some churches while you're out there."

"Huh?" I was kind of taken aback by this. I guess she was even *more* upset about the preacher last Sunday than I'd thought. Plus, with no kids to be a good example for, I'd planned on sleeping in on Sundays.

She looked at me seriously. "You could try out some different denominations and tell me about them. Maybe even the church you were brought up in. I can't change churches here, because everybody would know, and I don't want to make them feel bad. Besides, going to another church here would confuse the kids, and I like their Sunday school teachers. But if we moved, that would be different."

As she'd spoke, I'd realized this wasn't going to be something I could get out of easily, so I conceded. "Sure. I can do that."

She wouldn't appreciate a Havens or 'The Change' T-shirt but this was a gift she'd value. I could do our research, out from under the eagle eyes of the church members who watched her grow from a child to an adult with her own children, and maybe we could find a church with more meaning to her than history and worked better for me.

She gave me another quick hug. "Thanks. And I'll miss you."

"I'll call you when I stop tonight," I promised.

She nodded. I turned back to the kids, knelt down, and gave them another hug. "I'll miss you guys. Be good for your mom. And we'll skype as soon as I get to a place with decent internet." Thank goodness for technology; I'd still be able to see and talk to my family.

As I stood and turned to the car, Beth cleared her throat loudly behind me.

"Yes?" I asked as I hurriedly went through a mental checklist of what I could have forgotten.

"Don't tell me you seriously are wearing that? I thought you'd go into the house to change before you left."

"What?" I looked down at my favorite Superman T-shirt, my most comfortable shorts, and sandals. Sure, they were a little worn... okay, maybe a lot worn, as in, I'd rescued the shirt and shorts from the garbage a couple times, but, heck, a man had to have his comfortable clothes, and these were them.

"Don't you 'what?' me, Stanley."

The kids were beginning to snicker at me, which I knew was mostly Beth's reason for pitching a fit about my clothes, but only mostly, as she had thrown them out... more than once! "You can't be seen in public like that."

Playing along, I pretended to be offended. "There's nothing wrong with Superman."

"On a child, maybe."

I grinned. "Besides, who's going to see me? I'm driving for three days straight, and only going to talk to the gas pump and the drive-through speaker. What do they care about my clothes?"

Beth's playful expression changed. "I still don't feel comfortable with you sleeping in the car. It isn't safe. It's going to be hot so you're going to have to have the windows down at night. A stranger could walk up while you are sleeping. You should stay in hotels, so I know you're safe."

I looked at her. It bugged her I was doing it this way, but I didn't want to spend our severely limited money to sleep. I could sleep in the car perfectly fine, for free. The mood had been playful up to this point and I didn't want to leave with it anything different so I was careful with my words. "Once a stranger sees Superman sleeping in the car, they'll run away."

The kids laughed, and I felt much better, too.

In a staged-whisper, I said to my kids, "I'd better leave quick before she makes me go change." I leaned down and swept them into a quick hug and swatted their behinds to send them to their mother. I gave my wife a tight embrace and put my hands on each side of her face and looked deep into her eyes before kissing her. I then turned and hurriedly got into the car, slamming the door behind me.

I rolled the windows down as I started the car and waved as I pulled out of the driveway. A couple minutes later, I was around a corner with a smile on my face. A much better exit than I'd anticipated.

Man! I loved my wife.

# Chapter 3

About two miles down the mostly-empty subdivision streets, I was already on auto-pilot, effortlessly making my way to the highway, ignoring the wind blowing on me from my still opened window, focused on my thoughts rather than the road, sad about leaving my family, thinking about how long the trip was going to be, wondering how the job was going to be. As I felt the car slow, I snapped out of my trance and looked around the surprisingly deserted street, glad to see I'd endangered no cars in my distracted mental state. Slowing for the red light, I spotted a guy standing by the stoplight pole, knapsack at his feet.

When he saw I'd noticed him, he stuck out his thumb.

A long time ago, I'd promised Beth I wouldn't pick up hitchhikers. "You have a family that depends on you," she'd said. I think she'd watched too many late-night horror movies with serial killers and hitchhikers. There was a danger, I guess, so I couldn't argue with her, but I'd been on the side of the road with my thumb sticking out, watching the cars pass by too many times, and I knew the desperation a hitchhiker feels. But she'd asked, so out of a deep respect for Beth, I'd driven by many hitchhikers and tried to use Beth's logic of my family responsibility to lessen my guilt.

I slowed down more, hoping the light would turn green before I got to him. But the light seemed very fond of the color red and didn't change for my benefit. I knew I'd have to stop right in front of him. I debated rolling up the passenger window, but he was too close, and it would look very obvious what I was doing.

As I came to a stop, I went with my usual plan: don't make eye contact. Except something about him drew my gaze, and it was too late. We made eye contact.

He was about my height and age, with light brown hair just long enough to blow a little in the morning breeze. It looked like he hadn't shaved in a few days but he looked clean and well-groomed. He wore worn jeans and a navy T-shirt. Outwardly, nothing was unusual enough about him to draw my eye, except his smile. Never before had I seen a smile that felt so much like peace.

"Excuse me, friend," the man said as he stepped towards my car and leaning down to look in the window, "is there any way I can get a ride? I'm heading to Bethlehem, Pennsylvania. If you could drop me off any place in that direction, it'd be great."

Crap! I thought. Of all the cities he could be going, he was going twenty-seven-hundred miles, across the whole width of the continent, to the same city I was going to. What were the chances?

I debated lying, but I suck at that.

I glanced at the light; it was still red, even though I was the only car on the road. Usually this light turned green as soon as somebody pulled up to it. The light indeed seemed especially partial to being red today. Maybe it was broken.

I turned back as the man leaned down waiting for my reply, and I desperately tried to come up with an answer that didn't make me sound like a total jerk.

"I can pay for the gas," the man said, still smiling that peaceful smile, "for as far as you can take me. I'll even buy lunch."

Heaving an exasperated sigh--the one Beth assured me was where Cooper had learned his--I caved. "Sure. Throw your backpack in back." Man! How was I going to explain this to Beth? The gas money would be nice, but it wasn't worth violating Beth's trust. I'd have to drop him off as soon as I could.

The man's smile grew if that was possible. It was a little unnerving. Normal people didn't look that happy. "Thanks, friend," he said as he opened the backdoor and worked his backpack into my mess. From the size of his pack, he must have been planning on hiking for a while. He then hopped in the front seat and closed the door with a gentle hand.

As I glanced up at the still-red light, I wondered what kind of person says "Thanks, friend"? People don't say that kind of thing to strangers. Before I could think about that further, the light finally grew tired of being red, so I muttered, "No problem," as I started letting the clutch out and giving the car a little gas and desperately tried to figure out what I was going to tell Beth.

"This is great," the man said as he buckled his seatbelt. "I'll pick up the lunch tab if you can take me at least that far."

"It's no biggie," I replied, my mind already trying to devise a plan to get rid of him.

He looked around the car a little bit and at my two months' worth of stuff crammed in the back. "A Jetta Turbo Direct Inject. If you're traveling as far as it looks like with all the stuff in back, you'll be glad you have this car. What do you get? Forty miles per gallon?"

I thought, "Not a bad start, mister." He had hit on one subject I loved to talk about, cars and especially my TDI, but I wasn't going to get to know him on a personal basis because he'd be gone as soon as I could get him gone. There's no way I was going to talk about my trip or where I was going no matter how strange it was he was going the same place as me. But we could talk about my car all he wanted.

I followed his question with my own. "You a TDI fan? Not many people know what TDI stands for and most people, once they know it's a diesel, want to make the 'D' stand for diesel."

He nodded. "I'm a car buff, friend, and a buff of almost any other type of technology. VW did a nice job with this engine. A lot of people where I work out east have TDIs. Some of them have over three-hundred-thousand miles, and they're still going strong."

Following my plan of not getting to know him on a personal basis, I let the questions like 'where do you work?' and 'what do you do?' go unasked and worked to keep the conversation on a superficial level. "I'm hoping to get that kind of lifetime out of this. Once this is paid off, I never want another car payment."

Again, he nodded. "Great plan."

I didn't respond, and we were quiet for a minute.

He must have sensed my uneasiness. "Thanks again for picking me up, friend. Drop me off whenever you feel the time is right, and in the meantime, I'll try not to impose on you. I know how it is to pick up a stranger and then regret it because the guy won't shut up." He twisted in his seat, pulled a paperback from his pack, straightened, opened the book and began to read.

Interesting, I thought. Nicely played. Appreciation, but not gushing, and consideration I might not want to chatter the whole way, along with an obvious method of keeping himself occupied so I didn't feel obliged to entertain him. I hadn't planned to drop him off in the next few miles anyway, but now, I might let him buy me lunch someplace where he could easily pick up a new ride.

\* \* \*

I'd been driving for about thirty minutes or so, we were past the outskirts of town and into the desert, which would be our monotonous scenery until we hit Vegas. A little bit ago, I'd decided I'd take my hitchhiker as far as Vegas. He'd offered to pay for gas, and if he kept his word, that would save me some money. From there, he'd be able to find a more comfortable ride east, as there wasn't room in my car for two of us to sleep, and I definitely wasn't springing for hotels for the sake of a hitchhiker's comfort.

True to his word, he didn't push conversation and seemed content to read, glancing up on occasion as I passed another car, or to adjust the sun visor as the road changed direction.

We passed some roadwork warning signs and then saw the flagman holding the stop sign, sweltering in the summer sun, waiting for the exciting part of his job, when he got to turn the sign from 'Stop' to 'Slow.' But he didn't turn it before I reached him, so I was the first car in line. My lane was blocked by orange barrels, presumably for repairs of some type, and the oncoming lane was empty.

I waited patiently for a few minutes, but no cars came towards us and the line of cars behind us grew. Impatiently, I waited longer, grateful I wasn't the poor guy out in the sun, but still not happy. Out of frustration, I leaned my head on the steering wheel and mumbled under my breath, "It's a pretty good zoo."

To my astonishment, my stranger added the next sentence from the Dr. Seuss' *If I Ran the Zoo*. "Said young Gerald McGrew. 'And the fellow who runs it seems proud of it too.'" He looked over at me and winked.

That was pretty darn cool. No one ever caught that Dr. Seuss reference when I used it. Maybe this guy was all right. I continued the quotation, "'But if I ran the zoo,' said young Gerald McGrew, 'I'd make a few changes. That's just what I'd do...'"

He nodded approvingly. "I see you're a well-read guy."

"I've always enjoyed reading Dr. Seuss to my kids. You have kids?" I mentally winced when I asked, realizing that was a personal question and ran the risk of going past superficial.

"Yeah. I like reading to them, too."

I nodded approvingly, but it got me thinking about him. "Your wife doesn't mind you hitchhiking?"

The flagman finally reached the high point of his job and changed the sign to 'Slow'. I pushed in the clutch, put the car in first and followed the orange cones into the opposite lane.

While I was doing that, my passenger answered my question, "Not married."

I felt bad for asking but wasn't smart enough to quit. "Your kids are with your ex-wife?"

He shook his head but didn't seem bothered by me asking. "Never been married."

We passed big trucks working on the shoulder, and I started to ask the next questions, but quickly decided I was already past what I should be asking. I didn't want to get to know him too personally, as I wanted to drop him off as soon as I could.

Yet his answers got me more interested in him, and I looked at his worn athletic shoes and the almost-holes in the knees of his jeans. I figured I could safely ask a few questions without getting too personal. "So, why are you hitchhiking? Tough times or you got stranded out here?"

With the peaceful smile I'd already come to expect from him, he closed his book and turned in his seat so he could look at me. "My times are exactly as they should be, friend. And, no, I wasn't stranded. This is how I like to travel. I meet interesting people this way."

Finally, past the construction and back in my lane, I briefly wondered at the line-up of cars waiting in the other lane and what had been going on for so long when nobody had been moving. Then pushed the illogic of road construction aside and considered his answer. "Isn't it hard to get rides?"

He gave a small shrug. "Logic seemingly says so, as most people won't pick up strangers. But for me, rides always show up exactly when I need them. And they always turn out to be fascinating people."

I restrained a snort; maybe a 'fascinating' person would pick him up in Vegas.

As I passed a Mustang doing the speed limit, I asked, "You do this a lot?" While his clothes were worn and he was unshaven, he didn't strike me as someone who was down-and-out or a drifter type. Both he and his clothes were clean, and he was well-spoken with a hint of the east coast in his accent.

"I wouldn't say 'a lot,' but when I have to travel, I prefer this or my bicycle."

Had he misunderstood me? "Bicycle? I was talking about longer trips, like the one you're taking now."

"So am I, friend."

Why was he calling me 'friend' again? I'd only met him a half-hour ago, and we'd only had a few casual exchanges, so I certainly wasn't his friend. It was kind of irritating and a bit creepy. Curiosity over his bicycle trips wrestled with the friend-confusion for a few seconds, but curiosity won. "You ride your bike on two-thousand-mile trips?"

"Sure. Did it my first time when I was eighteen. It was what you'd call a *growing experience*." He shot me a self-deprecating grin. "But since then, I've found it's a great way to see the country and meet interesting people. When I take life nice and slow, instead of zooming by at seventy miles-per-hour, I can't help but feel a connection to the places I'm at and the people I meet."

I didn't restrain a snort this time. "But you don't get anywhere fast."

My hitchhiker nodded. "The journalist Charles Kuralt once said, 'Thanks to the interstate highway system, it is now possible to travel from coast to coast without seeing anything,' and he's correct." He looked past my shoulder for a long moment, presumably at the cars moving the other direction, then continued, "A number of years ago, I traveled coast-to-coast, in a car, by myself, because I was in a hurry to get where I needed to go. It turned out to be one of the most miserable times of my life. I sped right by everything and had no connection to anything. After that, I made sure if I needed to be somewhere, I gave myself time to travel how I like to travel."

"On a bike?" I asked incredulously. "I mean, yeah, a motorcycle would be okay, but a bicycle?"

"Yes, a bicycle. You should try it sometime," he replied with another smile. "You'd understand what I'm saying."

Beth would kill me, if I didn't kill myself in the process. All my jobs had me sitting at a desk all day and the only parts of my body getting exercise were my fingers on the keyboard. Then I heard the words coming out of my mouth, "It might not be bad..." Thankfully, reality caught up with my runaway mouth. "At least until it started raining, sleeting or snowing. Or I ended up here, in this god-forsaken desert, in the middle of a summer day."

My passenger sat quietly for a few minutes, staring out the windshield and smiling to himself. "There was one night I'll never forget. I was about twenty. About thirty miles from the closest town, I got caught in what Texans would call a 'gully washer.' I couldn't see far enough ahead of me to ride, and it was getting dark much sooner than I'd expected, so I staked my poncho over a barbwire fence in an attempt to protect myself from the downpour." He gave me another quick grin. "It didn't work very well. Water flowed under me all night."

I tried to imagine what that would have been like. It must have been impossible to sleep, and then to get up in the morning after being soaking wet all night, with nowhere to get clean or dry, and to have to face a thirty-mile ride to find shelter and food. "That must've been miserable!"

He looked at me with his peaceful smile and shrugged. "It's all part of the experience, friend."

I didn't know how to respond. My first thought was "Yeah, right. There are some experiences I could do without. Like getting laid off for five months and being scared out of my mind I wouldn't be able to feed my family." But, in a weird way, I could understand what he meant. It's all part of the experience *of life*.

In life, there's the good and the bad, the rain and the sun. I'd never thought about it in that way, nor had someone described it like that. Most people bitched and complained endlessly, they'd never quietly say, "It's all part of the experience."

After a few minutes of silence, my hitchhiker returned to his reading, and I contemplated my little revelation some more as I drove through the July desert, with the endless sun beating upon the car. Sure, sunstroke and sunburn might all be part of the experience of a long-haul bike ride, but right now, I was heartily grateful for the experience of a car with an air-conditioner.

Yet the more I thought about the statement, the more intriguing it was. In some ways, the things which had gone 'wrong' in my life had often forced me to change in ways that later helped me. I also thought about all the times I'd gotten extremely upset about something, only to later realize they were of little value. Taking his philosophy would have saved me much anxiety. It was an interesting thought.

An hour or so of silence followed. The expressway turned into a two-lane road and the truck traffic picked up. I'd expected both, since Beth and I had taken the kids to Vegas a couple times to see the sights.

Thinking of Beth right then must have triggered something because my phone rang and it was her. "Hey."

"Shouldn't the pool pump be on?" she asked.

I looked at the dash clock and tried to remember how I had set the timer. "No, it should come on in about an hour. Why?"

"Just wondering. There is stuff floating on top, and I noticed the pump wasn't running."

"It'll come on in a bit."

"Okay. Is the trip going okay?"

I glanced over at my passenger, who was quietly reading his book. She wouldn't be happy about me picking him up, yet with him right there, it wasn't time to get into this discussion, so I hedged. "No problems so far, but the trip is still young. There is plenty of time for things to go wrong."

Exasperatedly, she replied, "Thanks for the comforting words. Now I'll be able to sleep better tonight. Bye, Stanley."

"Bye." I put the phone back down on the center console and wondered how many calls like this I'd get on the trip and while I was out east. There were so many little things each of us did, and to the other person those things seemed to magically happen. I guessed there would be quite a few calls both ways. I mean, how does laundry get done, anyway?

As I approached the light at Kramer Junction, an oasis of fast food and truck stops at the intersection of two desert highways, I tapped my brakes as the truck in front of me slowed, and my passenger looked up from his book with a thoughtful expression. "Have you had your brakes looked at lately? I think they sound a little funny."

Putting my foot back onto the gas as the truck in front of me pulled into the truck stop, I absently answered, "I'd been meaning to have them checked, 'cause I think they're overdue. But money's been tight and they haven't started squealing, so I figured they could wait."

"Can you hit them a little? I should be able to tell," he requested. "I'm generally pretty good with cars being a," he did the air quotes, "'car buff' and all."

Since the light was red and I had to slow down anyway, I hit them with slightly more force than I might have otherwise. They sounded fine to me. I glanced at the light on the crossroad and saw it switch from green to yellow. I took my foot off the brake and downshifted, meaning to coast into the intersection as my light should turn green any second.

"A little harder," he said.

"Huh?"

"Hit them real hard for me. Just a quick test."

I glanced at the now green light and the clear intersection, then in my rearview mirror. Nobody behind me. *Fine, whatever.* I had been a little worried about the brakes, and if he knew cars, it was better to get them looked at in Vegas before I got into the endless fields of the country's midsection.

I stomped the brakes, hard, and the car shuddered to a stop on top of the white stop-line right as a motorcycle roared across the road in front of me at what must have been eighty miles an hour. If I hadn't tested the brakes, he'd have hit me dead-center of my door.

"No, they sound fine," my hitchhiker said nonchalantly.

With wide eyes and a pounding heart, I looked over at him, but he was already reabsorbed in his reading. Apparently, he wasn't aware how close to death I'd come. Sure, the VW was a safe little car, but getting directly smacked by a motorcycle going that fast was practically a death sentence in any car, and the motorcycle driver wouldn't have enjoyed the experience either.

Whacked, I thought as I carefully checked both directions, put the car into gear and stepped on the gas. The guy was seriously whacked. Then I muttered under my breath, "It's all part of the experience. Yeah, right."

# Chapter 4

I drove on, severely rattled by the near miss. As the desert miles passed, the sight of the motorcycle flashing in front of me kept playing over and over in my mind, and all I could think of was how close I'd come to making my wife a widow and my kids fatherless. What if I hadn't done what he asked, as I'd been tempted? It would have turned out so differently. I'd be dead, or close enough to make no difference.

Curiously, I looked over at my passenger as he calmly turned to the next page. It must be an astoundingly absorbing book to keep him that interested.

I looked back to the road and the thoughts continued until my cell phone rang, scaring me to death. I muttered to myself, "Superman's definitely lost his nerves of steel today," as I quickly grabbed the phone from the center console and placed it against my ear wondering what Beth needed help with. "What is it this time?"

"Ah, hello," the caller replied, in a hesitant deep male voice. "Is this Jeff?"

I pulled the phone away from my ear and looked at the caller ID, which showed a number I didn't recognize. "No, this is Stanley. You must have the wrong number."

"Jeff gave me this number and insisted I call him." The caller sounded rather upset and disappointed.

"Well, this isn't Jeff's phone, so he must have given you the wrong number. Sorry."

I was about to hang up when my passenger spoke up, "It's for me. I'm Jeff. I guess we never actually introduced ourselves." He reached for the phone, and after a moment, I handed it to him, not knowing what else to do.

I was dumbfounded. My mind was rolling over reason after reason as to how this hitchhiker got a call on my phone. Some led back to Beth's fear of hitchhikers stemming from late-night horror movies and occasional news reports of murders and hitchhikers. Some led back to my overindulgence of science fiction. But, as I listened to his side of the call, apprehensively watching him out of the corner of my eye, I dismissed those reasons. He didn't seem dangerous. But, then again, that's how many of the horror movies started off, too.

Jeff answered the caller, "Hey, friend." He paused for the reply, then said, "You finished the book? What'd you think? *Illusions* is one of my favorite books."

Talking about books. Seems harmless enough, I thought as I pretended to pay attention to the desert road while I eavesdropped.

"I thought you might like it," Jeff told the person on the phone. "It has that effect on a lot of people. I think you caught the point Richard Bach was trying to make perfectly. It's a life-changing perspective, isn't it?" Another pause. "That's great to hear, friend. Let me know how that goes. I'm positive it will work out even better than you expect." Pause. "Alright, friend, take care. I love you." He ended the call, handed my phone back to me, with a casual "Thanks" and went back to his book.

"Thanks?" I demanded, as I tossed the cell phone back into the console. "'Thanks' is all I get? I pick up a hitchhiking stranger--which my wife is going to kill me for, by the way--we almost get killed--which he doesn't seem to notice--and then he gets a call on *my* phone..." I sucked in a deep breath "and his response is 'Thanks'?"

He turned to me with that peaceful smile on his face and an amused gleam in his eye. "Thank you, very much?"

I wanted to be frustrated and angry, but I found that impossible to do when looking at him, so I looked back to the road and replied flatly, "Ha Ha," leaving the obvious question unasked. Beth always said I was too non-confrontational. She was obviously right.

He chuckled, returned to reading his book, and we drove on in silence.

As I pulled on to the ramp about a half-hour later to merge onto I-15 outside of Barstow, my hitchhiker--Jeff, I repeated to myself, because I'm horrible with names--spoke up, "You ready for the lunch I promised you? This town is the last place to stop for a while."

"Huh," I answered, as a semi tried to sideswipe me. Given the size of the truck and comparatively minuscule size of my Jetta, I backed off and let the truck have the lane. Then I reprocessed Jeff's question. Lunch? I'd forgotten his offer to cover lunch and gas. It was nice of him, but I wanted this trip over with as soon as possible, and I had sandwiches in the cooler and didn't want to waste the daylight, even if he was paying. "If you're hungry grab a sandwich out of the cooler."

He glanced at the cooler then back up at me. "We can eat those later. I promised you lunch and there's a great home-cooking type of restaurant a couple exits up here."

"Jeff," I said with a sigh, "if you want me to let you off here, I will. But I don't have time to stop at a sit-down place to eat. I've got a ton of miles to cover today."

"It's all part of the experience," he reminded me.

I passed another Jetta, a couple years newer than mine, then swung back into the right-hand lane. "If you want it to be *your* experience, that's cool. Tell me where to drop you. But *my* experience requires I keep my butt in this seat and on the road until about ten o'clock tonight."

"You're in such a hurry," he said, shaking his head in gentle reprimand. "You miss out on so many experiences of life."

"Yeah, well, that's life."

He shrugged, his smile never wavering. I think I could have stopped the car in the middle of the highway, told him to get out and he would have smiled and gotten out. After a bit he simply said, "Well then, yeah, drop me off at the restaurant. I'm not going to miss a good meal. It's this next exit."

Part of me was relieved because I wouldn't even have to take him to Vegas, but another part was hoping for his offered gas money, as anything he paid toward gas was more I could pay on my mortgage. But I wasn't the type to bring it up. "Fine." I pulled onto the exit ramp and followed it to the light. "Right or left?"

"Right, and then left into the restaurant across the street." He pointed.

"I see it." I followed his directions and a minute later pulled into a parking spot in front of the door. "You going to be able to find a ride from here?"

"Of course," he replied as he opened his door and let in a blast of desert heat. "But since we're here, why don't you come in. I'll buy you lunch, and you can save your sandwiches for later."

Now that I wasn't driving, I took a better look at his expression, then the smell from the restaurant that was wafting in his open door registered, suddenly making my cold sandwiches less appealing. "You're not going to let this go, are you?"

He smiled his annoying, peaceful smile. "I won't force you, but if you stay, you'll find it worth the delay. You'll like the food here."

I shook my head. Like with the semi on the highway ramp, I knew I'd been beaten. "Fine. Whatever." And shut off the car with an angry twist of my wrist.

"Thank you for keeping me company," Jeff said with sincerity.

"You're buying."

"Of course. That was our deal."

We got out and walked into the restaurant, which was obviously a family-run place, not a chain. He had been good-natured to this point so I decided to push him to see how he handled my idea of humor. "I eat a lot."

No change in his expression. "No problem."

"I eat a lot of the most expensive stuff on the menu," I said, still trying to be vague as to whether I was joking or serious.

Still smiling. "I may join you."

"I want a dessert. Maybe two."

Instead of being annoyed, he turned to me with a grin and exclaimed, "Awesome! They have the best blackberry cobbler here you've ever tasted." He paused as we waited inside the front door for the hostess to notice us and then added, "In fact, I may forego the lunch and have two helpings of that."

Realizing I'd been beaten at my own game, I gave up and looked around.

The restaurant was decorated in bright colors, and contained a cheerful but muted crowd. A beset looking waitress in her mid to late twenties with her dark blonde hair pulled back in a ponytail waved us to the last open booth in the far corner of the place.

I followed Jeff as he wound his way through the tables, and I watched the people react to him. He must have been smiling his smile because people glanced at him, looked startled and quickly turned away, then slowly looked back at him questioningly. I thought back to the first time I saw him, at the stoplight pole. He was a hard guy not to notice, yet he didn't do anything to draw attention to himself. Suddenly, I felt less like a schmuck for letting him buffalo me into eating here. The guy had a way about him that was hard to resist.

As I slid into the booth, another waitress dropped menus on the table and was gone before I could thank her.

"If you don't mind, may I order for you?" Jeff asked as he opened his menu. "I've been told I have a gift for knowing what people like."

Shaking my head, I said the only thing I could say. "Sure. Go for it."

He smiled at me, then up at the tired waitress who'd waved us to the table, whose name tag read 'Sally.'

"You ready to order?" she asked, not looking at us.

I crossed my arms on the table and watched the tableau play out.

Jeff didn't answer, only smiled at her.

Pen poised over her order pad, she looked as if she would break at any minute, the weight of the world heavy on her worn shoulders.

Jeff waited.

I smiled as I watched him watch her. He wasn't going to let her not notice him.

After a brief moment, she gave an exasperated sigh, opened her mouth to speak, and finally really looked at Jeff for the first time.

His smile grew; it was still a peaceful smile, but somehow *more* peaceful than the ones he'd granted me. He was something to watch in action with people.

"Hi, Sally," he said to her in his calm voice.

Sally obviously wasn't quite sure how to respond. She gave him a smile that was between forced and genuine, and in an unsure voice responded, "Hi."

Jeff continued, "And yes, Sally, we're ready to order."

She snapped her mouth closed and looked to me, confused.

I barely restrained a laugh as I shrugged and let my expression deny all culpability in the current events.

Sally turned back to Jeff and gave him another tentative smile.

Apparently, that was enough as Jeff finally ordered. He ordered me a patty melt, onion rings and a blueberry malt, and told her we both wanted the blackberry cobbler after we were done.

I had to admit, whoever said he was good at ordering for people was right. It wasn't at all what I'd have ordered, but after Sally walked away, I caught myself eagerly waiting for it.

The food arrived amazingly quickly for a restaurant this full, and when Sally brought it, her smile was much less tentative. Man! but the guy was good.

We ate in companionable silence. Maybe, I should have started some kind of conversation, but nothing came to mind, and Jeff seemed to be content to eat and look around. So, I quietly enjoyed my meal.

After the last bite of my patty melt, I finally vocalized my earlier thoughts. "Whoever said that about your gift for knowing what people want was right. That hit the spot like nothing else could have." I took another drink of my malt. "I can't remember the last time I had a blueberry malt. My dad used to take me to a place when I was a kid and this is what I ordered every time."

My thoughts drifted back to those special times, which were pleasantly interrupted when a bowl of steaming blackberry cobbler with a scoop of vanilla ice cream melting over it was placed in front of me. This started a new set of fond memories of picking blackberries at my grandmother's so I enjoyed my reminiscences as I ate.

As I spooned up the last bit of cobbler, Sally set the check on the table with another smile for Jeff, then she hurried off to serve other tables. I saw writing on the back of the check, so, being the nosey type, I turned it until I could read it. "Thanks for making--" the 'making' was underlined "--me smile. That helped more than you'll ever know. Have a safe trip to wherever you're headed. Sally Larsen." Somehow, I got the weird feeling Jeff already knew exactly how much his smile had meant to the worn-out woman. Looking at her again, she seemed too young to look so tired. I felt for her and briefly wondered what her story was, but let the thought pass. I'd never see her again and there was nothing I could do for her anyway.

I looked back at Jeff, who without even glancing at the amount for our meal, pulled two hundred-dollar bills out of his pocket and slid them under the check on the table.

I looked at him questioningly, but he wasn't looking at me. I finished the last of my malt and wiped my hands, before Jeff finally turned his focus to me.

"You ready to go?" he asked.

I nodded. "Sure."

As I followed him to the door, I looked back at the table with the hundred-dollar bills on it. Was he actually going to leave them there?

Outside, as I unlocked the car, he stopped at the newspaper rack and turned towards me. "Friend, you got," he looked back at the rack and back to me, "four quarters? I don't have any change."

He had bought me lunch, it was the least I could do. I held up my index finger to let him know to wait, reached in the car and grabbed some change floating around in one of the cup holders. I sorted through it for the quarters as I walked to him.

With a polite thanks, he took them and got his paper. He started scanning it as he slowly walked to the car.

I gingerly sat on the car's extremely toasty seat, wincing as it burned the back of my legs not covered by my shorts, and belatedly realized the justification I'd given Beth for wearing these clothes was shot. A whole restaurant full of people had seen my well-worn shorts and Superman T-shirt. Oh well. It wasn't the first time and wouldn't be the last.

As Jeff opened the door, I started the car and turned the AC on full blast, then waited for it to cool the car down enough that I dared close the door.

He had just slid into the passenger side, nose still in the paper, when the waitress, Sally, came rushing out, yelling, "Sir! Sir!" Jeff looked out, his still-open door. "Yes?"

"You forgot your change," she informed him, holding out a fistful of cash.

"No, I didn't," he answered. "That's your tip."

"But sir, you made a mistake. You paid with two hundred-dollar bills." She held the money out again, and I wasn't surprised when Jeff made no move to take it. "I didn't want you driving off and realizing your mistake later."

"There's no mistake," he replied in his peaceful voice.

Shock replaced her smile. "That's too much. I can't accept it."

"You don't need it?"

She stood there, the sizable tip in her open hand, looking at it with a bewildered stare. After several seconds, she said, "You're going to leave me a hundred and sixty-three dollar tip?"

"Yes," Jeff said in a matter-of-fact tone.

The car's AC had finally caught up with the summer heat, so I settled onto my seat and closed the door, still watching the drama unfold on the other side of the car.

Her bewildered stare went from the money to Jeff. "My electricity's supposed to be cut off tomorrow if I don't pay the minimum bill today. I wasn't worried for me, because I can make do, but my four-year-old daughter has asthma and the heat would be terrible for her without air conditioning." She looked again at the money she held. "And this is exactly what I need to pay so it isn't cut off."

With a casual nod, he answered, "Well, that worked out perfectly then. Do you need a ride to go pay it? My friend and I can take you there, if you'd like."

At this point, it didn't even surprise me this stranger had offered my car to take another stranger to pay her electric bill. It seemed to be a natural part of Jeff that he would offer.

After a short, stunned pause, she finally answered, "No. I get off in an hour and can go pay it."

"That's great. I hope the rest of your day is even better, friend."

He looked over at me as he closed his door. "You ready to go?"

I put the car in reverse and backed out of the parking spot. As I shifted into first gear, she came rushing up again.

I rolled down my window and she leaned down so she could see Jeff and ask, "How can I ever repay you?"

He shrugged. "If I have the opportunity to help, I help. That's all." He watched her as she obviously tried to form a reply, then he spoke, "If I gave you a book to read, would you read it?"

She blankly nodded.

I thought, "Here we go! He's some religious freak pushing his belief on vulnerable people." And for the first time, I took a good look at the book he'd been reading which was now resting on the parking brake between the seats and was surprised to see the front cover wasn't English.

Jeff glanced quickly at his book also and then to Sally. "You read German?"

She returned a look of "why are you asking me such a question?" but answered with a simple, "No."

"That's good because I'm not finished with this one yet. Let me get you another one. Would you mind pulling back in, Stanley?"

Even before I got parked again, he was turned around, kneeling on the seat, pulling books out of his sizable backpack, looking at each one before he set it aside. He then backed up in the seat enough to look through the window up at Sally from his backward position and asked, "Do you read only English?"

She timidly nodded.

Jeff hurriedly opened the door and looked at me as he got out. "This'll only take a minute."

I was torn between resigned and amused as he jumped out of the car and rushed back into the restaurant. I opened the door and stood beside the car. The waitress and I exchanged the same puzzled look as to why he went into the restaurant for a book.

Not wanting to stand in the excruciating parking lot heat, we followed him into the restaurant as Jeff proclaimed to the busy place, "I need to buy a book. I'll pay a hundred dollars to the first person who'll give me a book."

At first, everyone was silent and still, as the full restaurant looked at the man addressing them. Then everybody started looking around like there may be a book laying next to them they forgot they brought. Back in the far wall, near the corner where we sat, an athletic-looking high-school-aged boy with a T-shirt from his school's football team was sitting by himself. He opened his backpack and pulled a paperback out. Nervously, he asked, "Will this do?"

Jeff hurried over to the kid, and as he was reaching for the book, he asked, "What's your name, friend?"

"Harris," replied the boy.

The restaurant was quiet as everyone watched the scene unfold.

Jeff looked at the book, and if possible, an even bigger smile came across his face and his eyes lit up even more. "Are you sure you can part with it?"

With a confused look, Harris said, "It's a book from my summer school English Lit class; of course I can part with it. For a hundred bucks, you can have *all* my books. Won't need them anymore, anyway. Just need gas money."

Jeff looked at the aspiring football player for a second as if the kid was speaking a foreign language, then pulled a hundred out of his pocket and handed it to the boy. Looking away for a moment, Jeff shook his head as if to clear out the strange message. When he turned back to the restaurant, he was wearing his normal smile and he excitedly rushed over to Sally and asked, "Can I borrow your pen?"

She took a pen from her apron, handed it to him. Jeff opened the book, wrote several lines in the front cover, then handed both the pen and book to her saying, "*A Tree Grows in Brooklyn* is the perfect book for you. There *is* a tree growing in Barstow."

He hugged the completely bemused woman. "Bye, friend. I'll have to eat here the next time I'm in town. I like this restaurant." Then he turned and looked at the summer-school kid who'd supplied the book, and the same confused look crossed Jeff's face.

I wished I could tell what Jeff was thinking. Apparently, the boy puzzled Jeff, and even in my short time with Jeff, I knew this was a rare thing. He seemed to read people in the same way he read his books.

With another quick shake of his head, he returned to normal, his normal that is. "Ready now, Stanley?"

Almost expecting something else to stop us, I followed him to the car, and was mildly disappointed when we headed out and got back onto I-15 without interruption.

# Chapter 5

As we drove along, I watched the desert landscape roll by with power lines in the distance, and replayed what happened at the restaurant. Then as we passed a sign saying Las Vegas was forty miles ahead, I wondered about my passenger. I still planned to drop him off in Vegas, and my thoughts alternated between how to do that and back to the restaurant.

My phone broke the thought cycle. Thankful for the distraction, I quickly snatched it off the console to check the caller ID, hoping it was Beth, as I'd had enough strangeness today. But it wasn't her number, it wasn't one I knew, and wasn't in my contact list. "Hello?" I answered tentatively.

"Hello, Jeff?"

No way was this happening!

"Just a minute." I frowned and handed the phone to him.

He smiled and took it. "Hello, friend," he answered. "Yes, of course I remember you, how could I forget? That was quite a mess you were in. Did it work out okay?" He waited for the reply. "That's good to hear. I knew you'd make the right choice." He paused again. "Oh great, you did read the book?" Pause. "Yeah. *Stranger in a Strange Land* is an awesome book. Heinlein makes you think, doesn't he?" Pause. "Well, that's great news. I look forward to hearing how the rest works out." He ended the call and laid my phone back on the console.

I propped my elbow on the window and leaned my head on it as the monotony of the desert road stretched before us. The first time my phone had rung with a call for him, I was too muddled to even know how to respond, but this time I had to say something.

Keeping my eyes on the road, I asked, "How come, and *how*, are people calling you on *my* cell phone?"

"I don't have a cell phone," he replied with a casual shrug. "Hey, you said you had sandwiches, so I assume you have something to drink."

That actually sounded pretty good. "There's some Dew in the cooler back there. Help yourself," I said, straightening my head and shifting my numb butt in the seat.

"You want one?" he asked as he turned and opened the cooler.

"Yep, but you aren't getting out of answering my question. I'm not falling for the redirection."

"Darn! I thought it'd work." He turned back around with two Dews dripping from the melted ice. Once he'd put the cans in the cup-holders and buckled his seatbelt, he continued, "For me, it's about connections and distractions." He popped the top of his can and took a drink. "I like to focus on each moment I'm in. James Allen called it 'The Eternal Now.' Cell phones, especially ones with tons of functionality, bring the rest of the world into my moment, and I find it detracts from my experience of that moment." He glanced at me with a wry smile. "I love technology, though; I'm a big gadget fiend."

Letting the weird philosophy slide because that wasn't what I wanted to know, I asked, "Okay, but how are people calling you on *my* cell phone?"

In the matter-of-fact way I was getting used to, he said, "I gave them your number."

The guy was impossible. "Dang it, Jeff! Quit playing games with me. What's up? How'd you get my number? You stalking me or something? Like some serial killer playing with his prey?" I'd meant the last sentence as a joke, or maybe not. I'm not sure. But as soon as I said it, I realized how bad it sounded and swore I'd never watch another late-night horror flick with Beth. I'd been with the guy for a grand total of--I glanced at the clock and counted--five and a half hours, and didn't have enough rapport with him to exercise what my wife assured me was a questionable sense of humor.

But typical Jeff, he wasn't bothered and was going to enjoy every moment he was in. With mock-seriousness, he replied, "Maybe. We'll have to see how this plays out." Then turned and looked in the back of the wagon area. "You didn't leave much room for a body back there, did ya?"

Again, exactly like the highway ramp, I was a Jetta competing with a semi-truck. I dropped the whole topic and drove.

\* \* \*

As we hit the outskirts of Las Vegas an hour later, I saw the flashing lights of police cars a ways ahead. As I got closer, I could see they'd blocked off the road and were detouring people onto the exit ramp.

"Must be an accident," I muttered.

He looked up from his book but said nothing.

I navigated the detour onto the service road. The cars ahead of me had slowed to a crawl giving me time to be irritated at the delay or focus on more productive thoughts. I resumed trying to figure out how to politely kick him out, but when nothing feasible came to mind, my thoughts returned to the restaurant.

As traffic picked up some, I decided to try to get an answer out of him. "Pretty wild. Back at Barstow, you happen to pick a restaurant, where you offer to order my lunch, then you leave a ridiculous tip and it works out to the exact amount she needed to not have her electricity shut off. I mean, what are the odds?"

He looked over at me with his piercing smile. "I'd say it's close to impossible."

I was deeply annoyed with his response, or confused; I'm not sure which, probably both. "Normal people leave tips of fifteen percent and if they're extremely nice twenty-five percent! They don't leave three- or four-hundred percent tips!"

"So, what I did was wrong, friend?"

"No, not wrong, just not normal." *Man, I should learn to filter what I'm saying.* I called this very strange hitchhiker, one who didn't deny being a serial killer, 'abnormal.' *Beth is going to kill me if he doesn't.* "What I mean is..."

"Are we going to start talking about what's normal and what

isn't? Seems like a deep conversation for two friends who just met."

Now, I was beyond annoyed. "Strangers!"

"What?" he calmly asked.

"People who just met are *strangers*, not *friends!*" My tone was sharper than it should've been, but this guy was getting to me.

"I disagree," he said with the same unruffled tone and unnatural smile that had never left his face, except in that one instance with the high school kid at the restaurant. "Everybody I meet and spend any real time with becomes a friend of mine, so I skip the whole uncomfortable stranger step and move right into friendship."

"Everyone?" I almost yelled as I glared at him.

Calmly, and still with the unrelenting smile, he replied, "Yes, everyone."

"So you've never met someone who doesn't like you? You've never met someone you don't *like?*"

"For the first question, my new friends, people I just meet, people you'd call strangers, yes, they sometimes feel uncomfortable with me, much like you do now."

I winced.

"But that changes quickly. For example, they'll start forming a plan to relieve themselves of the discomfort. Maybe, they'll try to make up a white lie so our relationship won't have a chance to develop. Much like you've been doing."

He said it without judgment or any other negative inflection, but I winced again anyway.

"But that doesn't happen. Before they can sabotage the relationship, a true friendship's formed. For the second question, I meet people I don't agree with, but under all of their anger, hurt and broken dreams, or whatever separates us, is a person who is my friend. Those friendships actually form quicker than the first set."

His response made me angry, but I didn't know why. It might have been that he pegged me in the first group so well. Since he seemed to anticipate my plan for ditching him, I was getting less worried about being nice to him. "So, the angry ones instantly change for you because you're such a nice guy?"

I was at the verge of yelling, but his temperament didn't change. "Oh, I wouldn't say instantly. If you know what to say, what their problem is and can talk to them about it, they can change pretty quickly."

"People don't change quickly!" I sneered. "That's why psychiatrists make the big bucks. Because people need years of therapy to change."

He laughed softly, then asked, "Have you read the Bible? Saul changed to Paul pretty quickly."

I was so annoyed it took me a moment to realize I'd inadvertently wandered into the other lane because I was paying more attention to Jeff than the road. Valuing my neck, my anger stewed as I pulled off and stopped in a parking lot of a mostly abandoned strip mall, then quickly turned to my passenger. "Sure, if God is blinding you with a bright light and talks directly to you, I can see that changing someone quickly but..." I trailed off not sure where to go. I sure didn't want to get in a religious discussion with him.

He grinned and said, "Cool, we're in agreement then."

"What? No!" We needed to get back on track. "We're talking about you making friends with strangers, not God striking people with lighting."

"A flash of light surrounded him, not lightning." Jeff shrugged. "The special effects were good, but not needed. Just knowing what the problem is and what to say is usually enough."

Him bringing religion into our discussion aggravated me even more. I sucked in a deep breath to calm down and after a moment, more of our surroundings registered. The little strip of stores was mostly empty and we were the only car in the parking lot, but on the next corner a large bar was clearly doing a brisk business even though it was early afternoon. Its parking lot was about half-full, with hard-ridden motorcycles far outnumbering the battered cars and dirty pickups.

Wanting to prove my point, I said, "So, if you went in that bar right now, you could make friends with anyone there?" I pointed to a bar. It looked as inviting as I imagined Vlad the Impaler's house. Its sign simply read "Zack's." This wasn't a wanna' be weekend bikers' getaway. The bikes in front were monsters with plenty of hard miles put on them.

He looked over at the bar, then back at me with an amused gleam in his eyes. "Can I buy you a beer?"

Since he'd called my bluff, against my better judgment, I put the car in gear and pulled into the bar's parking lot. I'd always thought movies and TV make these places look worse than they were in real-life, but already I was reevaluating that opinion and wondering how I was going to explain this to Beth.

Jeff and I got out of the car, and we were hit with a blast of hot air. It must have been well over a hundred degrees out.

I looked down at my worn Superman T-shirt and ragged shorts, knowing they'd make me look even more out of place than I already did. I belatedly wished I'd listened to Beth and changed into jeans and a decent T-shirt like Jeff was wearing. With a silent "I should've listened to you" to my wife, I looked up and Jeff's hand was already on the handle of the dingy, black, windowless door. I mustered up all my courage and quickly caught up to him so I wouldn't have to enter by myself.

Jeff, however, seemed completely unfazed and walked in like he'd walked into the diner for lunch.

Well, I thought as I got my first glimpse of the interior, I was wrong. The movies didn't exaggerate these places. With complete disregard for whatever Nevada's laws were toward smoking in public places and OSHA sound regulations, I could barely make out the ceiling lights through the haze of smoke. The noise was deafening. Then the smell hit me. The smell of smoke was almost overtaken by the body odor of sweaty bikers riding in outrageously hot temperatures, old beer, and other things I'm sure I didn't want to know what they were. The place was dark, dirty and run down, about half the tables were occupied but my eyes were fearfully drawn to a gathering toward the back of the large room, about thirty tattooed, fierce looking men dressed in biker's leather... all staring at us.

My left foot took a step backward without conscious direction, and I thought that was an excellent idea. I'd let Jeff win this one without proof. "It's cool, 'friend,'" I said to his back. "You win. I believe you. You don't have to do this." I turned my Superman T-shirted-self around and left.

Back at my car, I opened the door, sat down, started it and cranked up the AC in almost one motion. Then I looked to the passenger door for Jeff to get in, but he wasn't there.

Confused, I looked back past the well-used bikes to the bar's door, only to come to the obvious conclusion he hadn't followed me out. He must not have heard me and was in there, by himself.

I sat for a long moment, sweating, not sure if it was because the AC still hadn't caught up, or from fear of going back in to get Jeff.

Actually, I was sure it was fear. After watching the unmoving black door of the bar intently for a minute, I resigned myself to the fact I couldn't sit in the car and leave him in there alone.

Mustering my courage, for the second time I headed into the cacophonous, odoriferous pit. After scanning the dimly lit room, I found him toward the middle of the bar, at a table between a waist-high wall that divided the room roughly in half and a line of unused pool tables. He looked small in contrast to the five huge bikers sitting at the table in front of him.

Jeff spotted me, and with an out-of-place smile, he waved his hand and yelled over the background noise, "Over here, Stanley! I saved a seat for you."

I swear, I almost cried. Jeff had said it loud enough everyone stopped talking and looked at me as the background music blared unaccompanied. Not only had he said it loud, he also hadn't said it in the manly way the protocol this type of establishment followed. I had never minded my name before, but in this context, it couldn't have sounded more unmanly.

Figuring the worse thing I could do in the eyes of this crowd was to bolt, I started walking to Jeff's table very conscious of my stride and gait, careful to avoid meeting the eyes of anybody in the place. It was the longest fifty-feet of my life.

Having passed the gauntlet unscathed, the noise level of the bar returned to normal as the bar's other occupants resumed their libations. My nerves were shot and I could barely support myself, so I placed my hands on the table as I moved around it causing the artificial wood-grained Formica table to wobble enough to almost knock over the two beers Jeff already had sitting there. For such a dive, this place had great service, I thought as I slid into the equally wobbly chair next to the dividing wall.

In a fashion I was starting to grow accustomed to, Jeff acted oblivious to the undercurrents of the situation. "I told you I'd buy the beer; you didn't need to go back for your wallet. I don't think they'll card you here, either."

In a fashion Jeff must be getting used to with me, I raised one side of my mouth with a look to indicate either contempt, confusion, or a number of other feelings that were not favorable towards him.

We sat sipping our beers without saying anything. It was a rowdy place and the table next to us, filled with monstrously sized men in old worn leather, was as loud as the rest, with profanity filling the majority of their sentences. But thankfully, no one appeared to be paying attention to us.

I started drinking my beer faster, hoping to get out of there soon, maybe before the loose ceiling tile I'd noticed above me fell.

Jeff leaned toward the table of monstrous men. "Hey, friends, would you mind stopping the swearing?" He said it still with the piercing unnaturally kind smile and eyes.

Five tattooed, scarred, massive men stopped talking and looked at Jeff and then me.

My heart sank.

Jeff took their sudden silence for compliance to his request. "Thanks, friends," he said, then turned back to me as if everything was normal.

Out of the corner of my eye, I watched the biggest, ugliest one, with his head shaved clean and a braided goatee to the middle of his chest, stand up, walk beside Jeff and tap him on the shoulder. "Excuse me, sir," the biker said in a very polite voice sounding more like a salesman than a thug.

Jeff looked up without removing his smile.

"My friends call me Bear. And your name is?"

"I'm Jeff, and this is my good friend Stanley," answered Jeff, and I wished he'd left me out of the introduction.

"Well, Jeff and Stanley, I would like to apologize for the

behavior of my associates and me. We're sorry we have offended you," Bear continued with a tone and vocabulary in total contrast to his look. With that, he lifted up his mighty hand, formed a fist, and connected it with the side of Jeff's face.

Jeff flew out of his chair and slid across the floor hitting his head on the leg of a pool table.

The giant then turned and took a slow step towards me.

Too scared to move, I just watched him.

"What about you, Superman?" he asked with fire in his eyes.

Out of pure fear, my bladder about to empty, I couldn't say a word. Then I saw Jeff get up.

"Wow, that was a great punch, friend!" Jeff exclaimed with an astounding amount of glee as he started toward us. Blood dripped from his nose and mouth.

In a rush of guilty relief, I watched the massive biker turn in amazement to the man with a bloody face and goofy smile.

"How's your left hand, Bear?"

After a few more sentences laced with the words Jeff requested the group not to use, Bear raised his left hand and made a fist, as Jeff stood relaxed with his hands at his side. Bear stood there, obviously confused by Jeff's inaction.

Jeff remained relaxed as he said, "I asked you not to speak like that. Not only is it offensive to me but it makes you sound stupid. Is that why you're so angry Bear? Did your father think you were stupid?"

I cringed and tried to formulate a plan to save Jeff which wouldn't end up in my own death. Nothing came to mind. Then I remembered the conversation in the car, and as the giant's left hand raced towards Jeff and landed solidly on the other side of Jeff's face, I wondered if these were the type of words Jeff had referred to, the ones that would change someone instantly. If so, I thought, maybe Jeff should re-evaluate his therapy technique.

Jeff staggered back about three steps but didn't fall, then nodded as if he'd figured something out. "Your left-hand's nowhere near as powerful as your right." Blood was now dripping out of both sides of his mouth but he was still smiling. "I think it's mostly due to your stance and form. With your right arm you're using your body, getting a lot of power from your hips."

Much like I'd seen Cooper's karate instructor do, Jeff changed his stance and rotated his hip, slowly demonstrating what he was talking about. "But with your left arm, you're relying on the power of your arm. See, like this." Again, he showed what he meant. "You see the difference?"

The sudden silence distracted me, and I looked around. The bartender must have turned off the music, and the other patrons were on their feet, coming to watch the festivities.

I turned back. The brute stood with a perplexed look on his face, which I totally understood, because this average-looking guy, smiling like a madman, with blood dripping onto his shirt, was critiquing Bear's form.

The crowd formed a large circle amongst the tables and pool tables, with Jeff and Bear at the center.

The biker shook his head, shaking away his disbelief, and again with a string of profanity yelled at Jeff.

"Friend, I'll ask you again to quit using language like that. It really does make you sound stupid. You never did answer my question. Did your father think you were stupid? You couldn't live up to his expectations? Do you talk to your mother that way?"

I sank further into my chair. I wouldn't have to worry about ditching my hitchhiker after that statement. I'd need to find a funeral home.

Bear's shaved head turned completely red. "Don't ever talk about my mother!" he threatened through clenched teeth as another swing connected with Jeff's face.

Jeff staggered back a couple of steps between two pool tables.

The crowd moved back and I leaned forward.

Bear took the same two steps forward towards Jeff and said something so laced with profanity it took me a bit to gather its meaning. As the biker landed another punch, pushing Jeff back more, I finally figured it out: Jeff wasn't allowed to mention the man who'd killed the biker's mother and if he did, great bodily harm would follow.

The crowd moved aside, to give Jeff more space past the pool tables, but was closing in front of me. I quickly stood and pushed my way to the front. As I'd watched the last few minutes, I'd realized, as implausible as it seemed, Jeff was in total control of the situation.

I saw the smile finally leave Jeff's face and saw more than heard him ask, "Your father killed your mother?" It didn't even look like Jeff noticed the punch following his very pointed question. The bikers in the splatter pattern did, though, as they backed away more.

Jeff's next sentence, "That explains a lot about your anger," was punctuated with another fist to his face.

I watched in awe. It was like a pop psychology show where the therapist was getting the snot beat out of him by a yelling and screaming client. Or like a movie where the guy goes to the gym and hits the punching bag over and over to deal with his anger. Except, Jeff was the punching bag, and the punching bag was hitting back with words. Every time Jeff said something to Bear, too low for the rest of us to hear, you could see Bear's reaction, and Bear was weakening.

Jeff was winning this fight without a throwing punch.

Finally, the massive man fell to his knees, placed his head in his hands and cried like a baby.

Jeff knelt down, putting his arms around him.

# Chapter 6

Realizing I'd quit breathing, I inhaled deeply. Jeff had done exactly what he'd said in the car. He somehow knew what the problem was and he knew exactly what to say. Being a human punching bag added to the effectiveness, though he took more of a beating than I'd have thought was humanly possible.

The awestruck bikers who formed the circle around them didn't know what to do. Jeff hadn't hit Bear even once, yet Bear was on his knees crying.

One of them finally gave an astounded and colorful exclamation.

Jeff looked up, his face bleeding and battered, but his expression serene with a touch of amusement.

The man said a simple, soft and solemn, "Sorry," and moved, with the visibly uncomfortable crowd, back toward their original tables and bar stools.

As the space around us cleared, Jeff looked up, his face swollen and bloody, and announced to one of the men from Bear's table, "Tell the bartender the next round is on me, friend."

The big, leather-clad biker turned away to deliver the message as Jeff stood with surprising grace, considering the beating he'd taken. He grabbed Bear's arm under his shoulder to help him up, which ended up being a strange sight in itself. By the time the huge leather-clad man finished standing, Jeff's hand was almost over his head. In a way, it reminded me of when Cooper "helped" me up when we finished wrestling.

"Let's talk some more," said Jeff to Bear, as he turned the man and headed to the back corner of the bar. He motioned me to follow.

I complied.

As we approached the corner table, its three occupants grabbed their drinks and moved without a word, the final man giving the table a cleaning swipe with a large handkerchief he'd pulled from his back pocket.

By the time I reached the table, Bear had sat and Jeff was leaning against a chair talking gently to him. At Jeff's insistence, I slid into the remaining chair.

Jeff looked to me. "I'll be right back. Going to go clean my face." With that, he turned and left.

I was left sitting with Bear, wondering what I was doing here at all.

I looked at Bear and he looked at me, neither knowing what to say.

Finally, Bear took the initiative. "Your friend is really something."

The tone of his voice was completely different. Its previous anger, harshness and bravado had been replaced by--I searched for a word. Humility? But I couldn't imagine the Bear I'd seen beat Jeff to a bloody pulp being the least little bit humble.

Then his words registered. *My friend?* The total of my time with Jeff was now approaching six or seven hours, most of them strange hours. But if I'd had to describe Jeff, "really something" was about as close as I'd get. "Yeah, that describes him pretty well."

I didn't know what else to say and was relieved when the waitress brought us the beers from the round Jeff bought.

Bear apparently sensed my discomfort, because he muttered in his deep voice, "Relax. I'm not going to rip your head off."

*Oh, like that reassured me.* But I nodded, gave a half-hearted smile and took a drink of my beer.

Bear didn't push the conversation and took a drink of his own beer.

We sat in awkward silence, sipping our beers, until Jeff came back a few minutes later.

Other than having washed the blood off his face, he didn't look any better. His face had started to swell, and a couple of the gashes were still seeping blood, for which he'd brought a few paper towels to hold on them until they quit. When the bruises colored up, he'd look even worse. Yet in typical Jeff fashion, he was oblivious to his appearance as he sat between us, the smile back on his face.

"Wow! That was something. I was beginning to wonder if you were going to quit," he said to Bear. His voice held not the slightest hint of malice or anger, if anything, his tone was complementary.

But obviously, Bear didn't take it that way, and he looked down at missing tiles on the floor, his expression filled with shame.

Without missing a beat, Jeff continued almost casually, "So, your father killed your mother? What happened? We didn't get to talk much about it a little while ago."

My pulse shot up as I readied myself to clear out.

It was obvious Bear's pulse also shot up, but he quickly got it under control. He went from looking at the missing floor tiles to looking up at the missing ceiling tiles.

I joined Bear in his evaluation of the place. It definitely needed some work. The background music had been turned back on at some point, but not so loud, and the rest of the bar's patrons were considerably more subdued than before. I caught more than a few of them sneaking hesitant glances toward our table. When Bear moved, I turned my attention back to him.

He took a drink of his beer, gave every visual cue he was going to say something and then quit, took another drink and thought for a minute. He then looked at Jeff. "I remember coming home from school; I was twelve years old. Had a bloody nose and maybe a black eye. My dad was home--he didn't have a job--and he saw me come in the door. He said 'The other guy'd better look worse than you!'" Bear grimaced, while shaking his head at the memory. "I should've told him the guy looked worse. The other guy was a couple grades ahead of me and bigger." He paused. "I should have told him I won. But I didn't. I confessed I hadn't been able to lay a hand on him. Dad threw his beer bottle at the wall, shattering glass everywhere, then gave me a second beating, this time, much worse."

Trying to imagine a father doing such a thing made me grateful for my father. It also made me value the relationship my kids and I had.

After a silent moment, Jeff asked compassionately, "Where was your mother?"

"She was there, at first, and then she left. When I noticed she'd gone, I was glad." Bear took another drink. "There was nothing she could do but make things worse for both of us. She'd done that too many times. When she tried to interfere, my beatings were worse, and hers were even worse than mine."

"Which hurt you more?"

Bear looked Jeff square in the eyes with the first hint of anger since the fight had ended. "I'd take his beatings all day if it meant he wouldn't touch her. She was beautiful. She deserved so much better."

"So, it was good she left," Jeff said, but I wasn't sure if it was a question or a statement.

Bear nodded. "It made it easier to take, knowing he wouldn't hurt her this time. Afterward, Dad stormed out of the house, and when I could, I went to find her." Bear sighed and looked at his beer bottle. "She was in bed, and I knew she'd been crying. She called me over and hugged me. As I'd walked into the room, I saw the bottle of whiskey next to the empty pill bottle on the nightstand and knew what she'd done."

He paused and picked up his beer, then set it down and with his fingertips gently slid it to the far side of the table. "I was happy for her, 'cause she was going to be free. I didn't call my dad or the police. She was finally going to be free." Bear smiled sadly. "She held my hand and told me she loved me. As we waited, she apologized over and over for not being stronger and for not being able to protect me. Maybe an hour or so later, she smiled at me for the last time, held my hand tight for a few more minutes, and then her grip relaxed. I went to my room, leaving her there. I remember being filled with so much happiness and rage, all at the same time."

After a pause he continued, "If I could've killed my dad that night, I think it would've been a perfect night. Mom went to heaven and my dad would've gone to hell." He gazed down at the table with a smile, reflecting his thoughts.

I took a towel from Jeff and tried to discreetly wipe my eyes.

Jeff waited for a few moments. "What happened next?"

Bear shrugged. "We had the funeral. My dad and I were there. That was it. She passed without the world knowing or caring." His expression changed to a confounded looking one. "Except for my dad. He noticed. He noticed her for the first time as he looked at her in that casket. He knelt beside the casket, crying like I'd never seen anyone do before. Afterward, he never drank another drop. Went and got a real job and even started going to church."

I looked at Jeff, but he was totally focused on Bear.

"How about you?" Jeff asked.

"Sure, I noticed," his face started turning red and his voiced raised, "and I know the mother--" he stopped with his top teeth pressed over his bottom lip in preparation to say the next word but he stopped and looked at Jeff. In a lowered voice, Bear continued, "I knew who killed her." He ran his finger over the spot in the table where the Formica was chipped. "He spent the next three years trying to be the dad he should have been all along. I spent the next three years hating him and fantasizing about ways to kill him. Then I left and never looked back."

"Where is he now?" Jeff asked.

"Last I heard, he was still here in Vegas. Spends most of his time with AA and his church. Never remarried. That was a few years ago. I don't know about him now."

Then Jeff floored me. "Bear," with which Bear looked at him, "it's time to forgive."

Bear studied Jeff intently and then replied softly, "You're right."

I was beyond floored. Astounded was even putting it mildly. The man who'd practically killed Jeff, who'd survived a childhood I couldn't imagine, who'd held his mother's hand while she died because of his father's abuse, had just said he'd forgive his tormentor?

Jeff simply said, "Call him."

Bear looked at Jeff. "It's been years. Home number's probably changed."

Jeff shrugged. "Give it a shot."

Bear pulled out his cell phone, looked at Jeff uncertainly, and then dialed. With a surprised look, he hesitantly said, "Dad?" He then got up and walked away to talk in private. After about two minutes, Bear returned to sit with us, but he didn't say anything.

I studied the man. He still had the gleaming shaved head and the braided goatee and still wore the dusty biker's leathers, but I realized he was a completely different man than the one who'd stared at us as we'd walked into the bar.

Saul had turned to Paul right before my eyes. I looked at Jeff in bewilderment.

He smirked and said, low enough Bear didn't hear, "I told you, you just need to know what to say."

There wasn't anything I could say to that, so I shook my head. Then a question occurred to me, a very uncomfortable question. Had I witnessed a miracle?

The waitress came, interrupting me before I could reflect more, and I ordered two beers. My last one had been gone for a while and I didn't want to be without one, again, then I thought about ordering a double shot of something. I'm not much of a drinker, but right now seemed like a good time for me to do just that. Before I could change my mind, the others ordered, and I left well-enough alone. Bear ordered water, which got a confused reaction from the waitress and Jeff ordered a Coke. Guess I was drinking alone, which didn't bother me a bit.

As she was about to walk away, Jeff stopped her, "Do you serve any food. I'm hungry."

She flatly replied, "Burgers and pizza."

"It's hard for me to turn down a pizza." He looked to me. "You want some pizza?" I nodded 'yes' in reply. "By the slice or do we need to order a whole one?"

With no more enthusiasm than before, she answered, "They're personal-sized. Cheese or sausage."

"Sausage for me." He looked at me and I nodded again. "Make it two sausages."

She walked off with no response.

Bear was visibly nervous as we sat there.

The conversation was light now, Jeff doing most of the talking, about the weather, the Vegas sights, and Bear muttering short answers to direct questions, which all suited me fine. I needed a break.

After a while, the pizzas were set before us and I winced. It looked like a seventy-nine-cent microwave pizza and the first bite confirmed that. Jeff looked as disappointed as me.

As we were finishing the last bites of the miserable pizza, I heard a sound outside of tires screeching on the parking lot asphalt, followed by the ominous sound of metal repeatedly crashing onto metal.

As one, the bikers jumped to check their bikes. They raced to the door only to become the pins of a perfect strike as they ricocheted off an impressively tall and broad-shouldered man, who bounded through the door not even noticing those in his way.

As the bikers around him staggered, the man scanned the dark bar with a look of panicked eagerness. Wearing khaki pants with a polo-style shirt and well-groomed hair, the man--Bear's father, I assumed--was a total contrast to Bear, and as ill-fit in this bar as Jeff and me. Once the man spotted Bear, he plowed toward us, the tables between us giving way with dull thuds and the crash of glass, as they were overturned. Given the size of this man and the determination with which he approached us, I thought the pool tables might give way, too, but he went around them, holding his intense and worried gaze on Bear.

Bear's father stopped in front of him, with a look of anxiety that would've made a brick wall cry.

The man who was no longer a brute slowly stood and faced the older man who'd made his youth a living hell.

If possible, the worried look on his father's face increased.

With the men standing face to face, it was obvious they shared DNA, both impressively large men and sharing heavy, muscular builds. Even with Bear's clean-shaved head and long goatee, contrasting his father's full head of well-groomed hair and a clean-shaven face, the father-son likeness was evident. The other thing which struck me was, in contrast to the ugly man I witnessed beat Jeff into his own submission, Bear's father did not share the ugliness. Yet, when I looked back at Bear, without his anger, his ugliness was no more; his expression was now gentle and longing.

Bear stood in front of his father, looked him in the eyes for a long time, with neither of them saying anything.

Finally, his father quietly and painfully asked, "Please, forgive me."

Bear looked into the watery, longing eyes of the man he'd spent so many years fantasizing about killing and put his arms around him. "I forgive you."

The father's knees buckled and he fell to the ground, helped down by his son, both crying.

After a moment, Jeff led them to our table and for the next two hours, I drank and they forgave.

Jeff said little, but the words he said were of a highly skilled craftsman guiding the tools in front of him, building a relationship that could not have otherwise existed.

After the tools were working without his guidance, he turned his bruised, swollen, and smiling face to me. "You ready to go, friend?"

Overwhelmed, I blearily nodded.

"But if you don't mind, I'm kind of whipped," Jeff said, then laughed, apparently thinking his own joke was funny. "There's a hotel up the road. Can we stop there for the night? I messed up your schedule today with this, so let me make it up to you by paying for your room."

"Okay," was all I could think to say, as Bear and his father stood to leave.

"Excellent!" Jeff cheerily clapped me on the back, then stood and turned to Bear, who walked up to Jeff and hugged him.

Jeff hugged Bear back, then let go, backed up, looked him square in the eyes and said, "I love you, friend," and then as if a thought struck him, "Hey, would you do me a favor?"

"Sure."

This was probably the most words the biker had ever said without a curse word, I thought as I tossed down the last of my beer, until Jeff got a hold of him.

"Would you read a book for me?"

Bear, now confused, answered again with a simple, "Sure."

Like he had at Sally's restaurant, in a loud voice Jeff announced, "I need a book. I'll pay a hundred dollars for it."

Unlike the restaurant, everyone sat still.

Jeff turned to me with a smile. "This may surprise you, but a book's going to cost me a lot more here than it did at the restaurant." Again, he announced, "A hundred dollars for a book, any book."

But again, they just sat there.

Jeff looked at me with even a bigger smile and turned to the room again. "A thousand dollars!"

Everyone sat there, until one older man slowly got up, trying to not be noticed, and started walking to the door. Then seven other men got up and tried to beat him to the door.

The man who got up first was the first one back in the bar, breathing heavily by the time he handed Jeff a well-worn copy of *Jubal Sackett* by Louis L'Amour. "I've had this book in my saddle bag for twenty years," he said. "I hate to part with it."

Jeff reached in his pants pocket and pulled out a massive wad of cash.

All I could think was this man was crazy to have walked into a biker bar with the largest wad of cash I'd ever seen.

He counted out ten hundred-dollar bills, paused, and then counted out two more and handed them to the biker. "I can't take something that valuable to you so cheap."

Jeff took the book, walked to the bar.

We followed.

When he got up there, Jeff asked the bartender for a pen.

The gray-haired, weathered bartender, wearing a black T-shirt with 'Zack's' in large white letters on it, looked deeply at Jeff for a long time. It was hard to read what the bartender was thinking as he studied Jeff with little change in his expression. Finally, without taking his eyes off Jeff, he reached down to the counter, picked up a pen and handed it to Jeff without a word.

Jeff smiled back at him as he took it. "You Zack?"

The bartender nodded in affirmation but still no words.

Out of the lips that were starting to swell, "Had a great time here tonight, friend," then he leaned in closer to Zack, slid a couple hundred dollar bills across the counter and in a hushed voice said, "Except for the pizza. You clearly need to work on that."

Zack emotionlessly scooped the money into the till, looked at

Jeff for a minute, then turned away and went back to his duties.

As in the restaurant, Jeff opened the front cover of the book and wrote something, then handed it to Bear. "Here you go, let me know what you think of it."

Bear, like it was the most natural thing he'd ever done, responded, "I love you." He looked over at his father then back to Jeff and followed up with, "Thanks."

Jeff turned to me. "You ready to go, Stanley?"

Jeff headed towards the door, turned to look at all the thugs in the room. He stood there looking like he just came out of a plane crash and said, "Had a great time, friends. You can be sure the next time I come through town I'll be stopping in and I'll buy the first round. Love you, guys."

No one said anything. They'd watched the biggest, meanest person they'd ever known hug this strange guy and tell him he loved him.

Jeff, with his unceasing smile, turned and walked toward the door.

"I'll be right out," I called after him.

As Jeff walked out, I turned to the man who'd threatened to kill me earlier in the evening and asked, "Can I see that book for a second?"

"Sure, friend." He handed it to me.

*What?* Did he just call me 'friend'? I shook that off and opened the front of the book.

> *Call me when you finish the book. Let me know what you thought of it. I can be reached at 661-555-6090.*

> *Do me another favor. Call 760-555-4212 two weeks from today. Tell the person you would like to set up a time to meet.*

Jeff had written my number in the book! I handed the book back, turned and started to the parking lot.

"I love you," called Bear after me.

I froze. There is no way that happened. I turned and looked.

He repeated the words. "I love you."

What could I do? "I love you, too." I turned and walked out.

# Chapter 7

Once I was at the car, Jeff asked, "Mind if I drive? You were putting them away pretty good, and I switched to Coke after the first one."

I was shaky from the experience, not the beer, but I agreed I wasn't in any shape to drive and tossed him the keys.

Jeff drove a few miles to a cheap hotel right off the highway, in the usual strip of other cheap hotels and restaurants.

I didn't want the police coming to question us because Jeff was so battered and covered with blood, so I stuck out my hand and he handed me some money. I went into the office, paid for two rooms and got back in the car.

He parked in front of the rooms, and I handed him his room key.

Without saying anything or even looking at Jeff, I got out, grabbed my bag from the backseat and went into my room. I wanted to go to bed and wake up back in my normal life, or wake up and realize it'd all been a dream.

The clock on the nightstand read just after six. Beth would be expecting a call later tonight, to let her know I was safe and where I was spending the night. What was I going to tell her?

She and I have always been honest with each other, so I wasn't going to hide this, but I wasn't quite sure what had happened today, so I had no idea what to tell her, let alone *how* to tell her. The fact that I'd picked up a hitchhiker was enough reason for me to delay calling her until I came up with better answers than I had now. What happened after I'd picked him up was even more reason to delay. I'd call in a couple hours, after I had time to think about the day. Time to think about whether or not I'd ditch my hitchhiker in Vegas like I'd originally planned.

With that one little thing settled, I stretched out on the bed, flipped on the TV and started clicking through channels until I found the Sci-Fi channel. That perked me up a little. Even better, the mid-eighties sci-fi movie *Starman* was on. I've always liked that show. An alien takes the form of a woman's dead husband, and the alien and the woman end up being chased cross-country by the government. They make it to Crater National Park so the alien could be picked up by his people before he dies.

After today's adventure, I felt for the lady in the movie. I now knew what it was like to be on a long car trip with a very strange man. At least Jeff and I weren't trying to outrun the government.

Unsurprisingly, my plan to have the movie distract me enough to reset my thinking process didn't work. The day replayed itself over and over until there was a knock at the door which brought me out of my daze.

Looking through the peephole, I saw a pizza man, which made me realize I hadn't eaten dinner, except for the awful pizza at the bar.

Leaving the chain on the door, I opened it a bit. "I didn't order anything."

The deliveryman responded, "The guy next door did. He said this was yours."

Good idea, Jeff, I thought, even though I didn't want to spend the money. I opened the door and said, "Let me get my wallet," and started towards the nightstand where I'd emptied my pockets.

He stopped me. "The guy next door paid for it."

Huh. Well, after today, maybe pizza was the least Jeff owed me. "Let me get you a tip." I continued towards the nightstand.

"Oh no, believe me, he took care of that, too."

At the thought of the hundred-dollar bills Jeff threw around like candy, I turned back to the door. "Okay, great." I took the pizza and drink.

As the delivery guy was about to leave, he said, "Your friend doesn't look so good. You might want to get him to a doctor."

For a brief second I was worried, so I asked, "Was he acting okay?"

"I don't know, but I don't think so. He acted way too happy for a guy who was beat up that bad. He might be kind of loopy. I mean, he gave me a hundred-dollar tip."

I felt better. That was his normal behavior from what I'd seen today. To make the pizza man feel better I said, "Thanks for letting me know. I'll check on him."

The deliveryman nodded, turned and left.

After eating a few pieces of mediocre pizza and finishing the movie, I felt much better. I hadn't realized how hungry I was. I was also coming off the effect of the beer and that always makes me tired. The drink and pizza were a perfect solution.

As the credits rolled, I turned off the TV. Even with a full stomach, the movie hadn't been the escapism I'd hoped for. Watching someone on a road trip with an alien had kept bringing my thoughts back to Jeff. But I felt better, and now I was ready to call Beth.

She picked it up after a couple rings. "Hey, Stanley."

"Hi, Beth," I answered, trying to sound normal. "I'm just checking in. Making sure you guys are doing okay without me."

"It's been tough so far, but Thing 1 and Thing 2 are hanging on." Then she whispered, "They're driving me nuts!"

I smiled. I knew they were right there listening because I could hear them laughing in the background. I glanced at the clock. I'd probably caught them all in our bed as she read to them before bedtime. "Well," I started off, "I have some good news and some bad news." This approach always worked.

I heard her put her hand over the phone and a muffled, "Kids, go put a movie on or something, let me talk with your Dad." After a pause, she said, "Stanley! I hate it when you do this. What happened?"

Her response let me know, once again, I was wrong and my approach wasn't going to work. So being blunt was my next option. "I've stopped for the night and am staying in a hotel."

"Oh!" was her surprised response. She knew me well enough to know I wouldn't spend money only to sleep unless something major was up. In a worried tone, she asked, "What's wrong? Is the

Jetta having problems?"

"No, the Jetta is fine, and well, I guess everything is fine. Just not how I planned on the trip going."

"Why? What's happening?" She didn't sound any less worried. "Where are you?"

"I'm a little outside Las Vegas."

"That's it? I expected you to be a lot farther along. That's going to make the next two days too long for you to drive. Or are you going to take an extra day?"

That hadn't occurred to me. "Yeah, I guess I'll have to."

"Why's that all the further you made it?"

"Well, that's an interesting story." I was kind of looking forward to hearing it myself, seeing if it made more sense the second time around. "As I was leaving the house, you know that first light as we leave the subdivision?"

"Yes?"

"Have you ever had to wait for it to change?"

Beth thought for a bit before answering, "No, I guess not. It usually turns green before I get to it."

"Right. It's always done that for me, too." And I went quickly through my day, soothing her ruffled feathers as best I could about picking up a hitchhiker. I told her about Jeff's crazy smile and people calling him on my phone. I told her about Sally getting the exact amount she needed at the restaurant, Bear's Saul/Paul conversion at the bar and his reconciliation with his father. I told her about some of the conversations we had and about Jeff's habit of giving away books. I told her as much for my benefit as hers. As I listened to the story I was telling, it didn't sound any less weird than when I lived through it. When I finally finished, there was a long pause.

"Stanley, it sounds like it'd be best to finish the trip by yourself."

I'd been pondering if I should get rid of Jeff all through the movie, so it was nice to hear her confirm my thoughts.

"Yeah, I know. He's a nice guy and all, but weird. And I suspect this would be a long trip with him along. So, yes, you're right." I was decided. "That's exactly what I'm going to do." I felt vastly relieved. I'd let him buy me a tank of gas, and drop him off somewhere in town where he could easily pick up another ride, and get on my way. I had a long few days' driving ahead of me and didn't need Jeff's hassles before starting a new job. "But in the meantime," I said to my wife, knowing my voice conveyed my relieved smile, "they have the Sci-Fi channel. I just got done watching *Starman*."

Exasperated, Beth said, "Again?"

We talked some more, and I talked to the kids for a little while, before I started fading. All the day's events, and the beer, were catching up with me. I told them all good-bye and hung up with a contented heart.

I got ready for bed, was asleep five minutes after my head hit the pillow and didn't move until morning.

\* \* \*

When I woke up, I lay in bed working through tactics for getting rid of Jeff. Maybe the best way was the coward's way; I'd load up my car and go. I couldn't handle another day like yesterday. And even though the guy wore scruffy clothes and only had a backpack, he threw money around like he was loaded, so at the very least he could call himself a cab to take him into a more populated area.

That was the plan until I had everything packed and was ready to go to the car. As I searched the room for my keys, I realized he still had them.

"Time for plan B," I muttered to myself, except I didn't have one. As I sat on the bed thinking, there was a knock on the door.

"Stanley, I filled up the car so you could sleep longer," Jeff called through the door in his normal calm voice as if nothing was askew. "You ready to get some breakfast?"

There was only one way to handle this and that was to be straightforward and upfront with him. I'd open the door and tell him he needed to find another ride.

I swung the door open, and there he stood, clean shirt and pants, freshly showered, and otherwise looking like death warmed over. His face was cut, bruised, and swollen, and his arms had black and blue marks up to his T-shirt sleeves. This guy wasn't going to get a ride from anyone. And I was a sucker. With a resigned sigh, I said, "Under one condition."

"Sure, friend, whatever you want."

His smile hadn't gone away overnight, and I was getting used to his constant use of 'friend.' Then his words registered. "Whatever I want?" I exclaimed. "How can you say that?" I searched for an extreme example. "What if I said we needed to kill the housecleaning crew?"

"*All* of them? Why not just the one responsible for not leaving me any conditioner? Your room must have been *way* worse than mine if you want to kill *all* of them."

It was useless. "Come on, let's go get breakfast."

"Without killing anyone?" questioned Jeff.

I laughed under my breath. "I guess not today." Then in a mock angry voice, I said, "But there'd better be conditioner at the next place."

We started walking to the restaurant.

It was obviously going to be another hot desert day, and I had a ton of miles to cover. I didn't have time for any more of Jeff's games. While we walked, I said, "There *is* one condition. You don't say 'anything.'"

"Sure, friend," he answered very seriously.

"You don't talk to anyone. I'll order for you, so you don't even need to." I was wondering how he'd take that.

"No problem. I won't say a word to anyone. Does that include you?"

"I'll have to think about that."

True to his word, he didn't say a word to anybody. At the restaurant, he got some worried looks from people due to how beat up he was, but no one said anything to him either.

I ordered breakfast for us both, scrambled eggs sampler plate and orange juice. When it came, he started eating it up, happy as a lark, smiling and chewing.

As I watched him, I couldn't stand it any longer; the questions were racing through my mind about him and the whole strange previous day. "So, what's up with you?"

"Can I talk now?" he asked, pretending innocence.

I muttered some very uncomplimentary things under my breath, which included some of the phrases Jeff had been so insistent Bear not use and then said, "Yes, but only to me."

"Great! What did you mean by your question?"

"Don't do that to me! You know what I mean. Yesterday was the most bizarre day of my life, and you act as if nothing happened."

"So, ask a more specific question, and I'll try to explain the best I can." He looked very serious. As serious as a guy with a smile that never ended and a bruised and swollen face could look.

Ask him a question? Where would I start? We sat in silence for a few minutes and ate, while I pondered that. Finally, I looked at him and then asked the most obvious question. "Doesn't your face hurt?"

"Oh man! It hurts bad," he said way too gleefully. "Bear had a great punch, once he put his hip behind that left of his."

I let the reminder of the boxing lesson slide. "But you let him hit you, over and over."

"Yeah, but I didn't let him do any real damage. See." He gave me a toothy grin. "I've got all my teeth and no broken bones. I let him take his anger out on me. Like I told you before we went in there, the angry ones become friends faster than others. Their anger's wearing them out. They're so ready to love; they just need to deal with their anger. Once that's done, the rest is easy."

"Why didn't you... we... just get out of there when we had the chance? Why'd you turn around and provoke him?"

He looked at me in shock. "What do you mean 'me provoke him'? He was the one swearing. I truly detest hearing people talk like that."

"We," I started to say very loudly but then caught myself before I drew everyone in the restaurant's attention. "We were in a run-down biker bar. Did you expect them to be reciting poetry or discussing how the policies of the current administration affect the socioeconomic status of the working class? We were in a bar! They were swearing!"

He nodded with a thoughtful look. "Poetry would have been cool, and as far as the socioeco--"

"Whoa!" I said stopping him, then with quiet intensity continued, "We were in a bar, Jeff!"

Letting his expression grow serious, he replied, "I'm here to remove the barriers holding humanity back."

*What kind of statement is that? What the heck did he mean by it?* I leaned forward to ask him, and he paused to let me do so. But as I thought more about it, I figured I'd misunderstood what he said and didn't want to bring attention to it. I couldn't think of what else to say, so I leaned back to let him continue, which he did.

"For example, humanity's command of language is one of the greatest gifts God gave us. Because of it, great societies have been formed, great advances in technology have been achieved, knowledge from our ancestors has been passed on to us, and beautiful literary works of art are here for us to enjoy. Imagine Shakespeare over-run with profanity. The art would be lost."

I thought about that. Being an English major, his example hit home with me; I loved Shakespeare and his artistic use of language. It also made me think about all the movies I'd wanted to enjoy, except the profanity detracted so much enjoyment I'd finally shut it off or leave the theater. "Okay, I guess I can see that to some extent, but again, we were in a biker bar, what do you expect? These aren't Harvard grads."

He looked out the restaurant window at a motorcycle passing and then turned back to me. "I talked to a teacher once. This teacher said she worked in a school which had a dress code her first year there, but the following year it was removed. She said the difference between the students, the exact same students, was stark between the two years."

He picked up his orange juice and took a swig, then continued, "When people dress nicely, they're more likely to act nicely. When they dress like thugs or hoodlums, they're more likely going to act exactly like they're dressed.

"The language people use is even more important. When people speak like uneducated idiots, they're less likely to push themselves forward in any direction that betters themselves. The people who will want to associate with them are not people who'll benefit them, help them grow."

I found myself nodding, as I remembered all the examples I'd seen in my life.

"'As a man thinketh in his heart, so is he,'" Jeff quoted. "The language a person chooses to use, or willingly listens to, is a great reflection of their potential."

"But isn't..." I stopped and tried to reform my thought. "Wouldn't..." Again, what I wanted to say wasn't forming in my head. *So much for my command of the English language.* I wasn't getting anywhere so waved to Jeff to continue.

"Our friend Bear will no longer be restricted by his limited language. Now, language will become a finely honed tool."

The waitress refilled our water glasses as she tried not to stare at Jeff.

I thanked her and took a drink, thankful for the distraction from Jeff. Who was this guy?

He took a drink and then looked at me. "Don't get me wrong. In the great scheme of things, profanity's trivial. Profanity has been around since language was invented and always will be. The *big* issue is that excessive and habitual profanity is a symptom of a problem humanity's had long before language."

I didn't like the weird way the conversation was going. All the talk about 'humanity' was strange. I didn't respond and took a drink of water to serve as a reason not to say anything.

He watched me with a curious smile, and after I couldn't drink anymore without being obvious, he asked, "You ever read anything by Karen Armstrong?"

Clearly, he was a big reader. I liked to read, but between work, family, and household chores, I didn't have much time for it. "No."

"She has a book called *Twelve Steps to a Compassionate Life*. In it, she says we inherited from our reptile ancestors some traits, like our interest in status, power--" he ticked them off on his fingers "--control, territory, sex, personal gain, and survival. These drives are based in the most primitive part of our brain." He stopped and picked his fork back up, giving me a chance to think about it.

The conversation was actually getting interesting. Plus, it helped he wasn't telling me evolution was an evil scientific plot to lead people to atheism and hell. I summed up my interpretation of his point. "So, the big problem's been around forever is, for most people, their thought process hasn't changed much from reptile times."

"Right on, Stanley. Excessive profanity is one symptom of a person being based in their reptile-brain rather than their higher human-brain. There's been some new research, which proves my point. MRI images show swearing is processed in a totally different part of the brain than other language. You want to guess where?"

I nodded. "From the same primitive region as all the drives you just mentioned."

"You got it. If you, me, and the rest of humanity wants to move past our reptilian ancestry, we'll need to quit exercising our lizard-brains and begin exercising our modern brains, our human-brains. The language we use, and listen to, is an easy starting point toward doing that."

That was cool to think about. I didn't get to have discussions like this very often; most people I knew blindly lived their lives, not thinking much past their day-to-day existence. As much as Jeff had read on this trip so far, my guess was he had a lot of knowledge about stuff like this. It might make for some interesting conversations.

I thought more, and he let me do so. He'd given swearing as one example, there had to be more to it. "What are some other things people can do to exercise their human-brains?"

He grinned. "You just did the biggest and best. Ask questions. Want to learn, and do learn." He shrugged. "It's simple. If everybody made a commitment to learning something new every day, this world would be a totally different place in a very short time."

"Hmmm," I replied.

"Beyond that, look at the words Ms. Armstrong used: status, power, control, territory, sex, personal gain, and survival. What if humanity replaced thoughts of 'status' with thoughts of 'compassion'? 'Personal gain' with 'for the long-term betterment of all'? 'Control' with 'cooperation'? And so on. The world would be born anew."

I slumped back in the booth, stunned.

He grinned unrepentantly. It was obvious he liked blowing my mind.

"It can't be that simple," I grumbled at him.

Giving a slight laugh, he replied, "Didn't say it was simple. Look how beat up I got stopping one guy from cussing."

I burst out laughing.

Jeff added, "Besides, words are easy, the actions are hard."

# Chapter 8

I raised my eyebrow in agreement, "Isn't that always the case?"

While taking a few more bites of breakfast and mulling over his points, my thoughts kept circling back to this strange man himself. I'd never met anybody remotely like Jeff.

Not only had I witnessed some extremely strange stuff with him yesterday, but everything about him seemed different. The way he carried himself, the depth of his smile, the certainty in the way he talked, and even the way he used money was different. He didn't look like a guy who had lots of money, but I'd seen him give it away yesterday like it was nothing.

Money was a subject which had bugged me for five months, well, all my life, really. Changing humanity seemed too big a topic to pursue more, I'd let that percolate for a while. Money seemed a little more my size, so that topic came out as my question. "You seem to have plenty of money, why are you hitchhiking across the country? Why don't you fly or at least buy a car and drive?"

Jeff finished chewing and then answered, "Didn't we cover that one yesterday? Where's the adventure in that, Stanley? I wouldn't have met you, or Sally, or Bear, or Zack, or those other nice people at the bar, if I'd done that."

He added matter-of-factly, "Oh, and you'd be dead," as he looked back down to his plate. Equally nonchalantly, he scooped a forkful of fried potatoes and ate it.

I simply stared.

After he finished chewing, he cut a sausage and put it on the end of his fork and then casually continued, "That motorcycle would've hit your door. Part of the rider would have come through the window and broken your neck, and the impact of the bike would have shattered your left leg and hip, but you'd have been dead already, so you wouldn't have cared.

"The part of the motorcyclist that didn't go through the window would have landed thirty feet or so past the car. It would've been a horrific mess." He paused to meet my flabbergasted gaze. "Would I've been a good person if I let that happen?" He put the sausage in his mouth and started chewing.

That wasn't quite the answer I'd expected, and I knew my mouth hung wide open. How could someone say all that with a smile on their face? How could he know that?

Snapping my mouth shut, I looked to the others in the tiny restaurant. With everything else that happened yesterday, I'd forgotten about the strange near-miss with the motorcycle. I hadn't even told Beth about it last night. I turned my attention back to Jeff, and in a sarcastic, sharp voice said, "So, you can predict the future?"

"Sure," he said with a negligent shrug.

Once again, that wasn't the answer I'd expected. I sat there looking at him trying to think of what to say next.

He broke the silence with, "Can I talk to someone now?"

I responded with an unsure nod.

"That is Sean walking through the door right now, he's an elevator technician."

I looked at the balding middle-aged man in a plain dark blue T-shirt.

Jeff continued, "A fire truck is going to race by. The cell phone at the table next to us is going to ring. It's his mother calling, wondering if they're coming over for dinner this weekend."

Jeff stood and walked to the man by the door. "Sean?"

The man, who had his back to Jeff, turned, apparently wondering who was calling him. Shock covered his face as he got a good look at Jeff, battered and bruised, and then his expression changed to confusion. "Do I know you?" he asked loud enough I could hear over the babble of the small crowd.

"Not at all," Jeff replied with his usual cheerfulness, "but it's great to see you anyway. How's the elevator business treating you?"

Still mystified, Sean answered, obviously out of habit, "Oh, it has its ups and downs." He laughed at his own joke and Jeff laughed with him.

"I want you to meet a friend of mine," Jeff said and casually turned back to our table.

The bewildered, but unresisting, the man followed.

Jeff introduced us and the confused man shook my hand.

When we heard the fire truck sirens, we all looked out the window.

"I hate to run out like this, Sean," Jeff said, oh so casually, patting the man companionably on the shoulder, "but Stanley and I are running late, and we have a long trip ahead of us."

Jeff put way too much money on the table, and as I stood to leave, I heard a cell phone ring. "Hi Mom.... Sure we can.... Do you want us to bring anything?"

Luckily, the guy on the phone didn't notice my astounded reaction. Jeff had batted a thousand, three for three. I looked toward Jeff; he was waiting for me at the door. When he knew I saw him, Jeff went out the door and toward my car. I followed, trying to make some rational sense of what had happened, leaving Sean staring after us.

My strange stranger kept getting stranger.

And it looked like I was stuck with him a while longer. Beth was going to skin me alive.

As I mechanically unlocked the doors and climbed into the driver's seat, I supposed that was one good point for living on the other side of the continent for the next couple of months. She couldn't skin me over the phone, and there was a slim chance she'd calm down by the time I got home.

* * *

The drive through Las Vegas was very quiet. Jeff read and I tried to recover my equilibrium. I barely remember seeing any of the town.

On the other side of Vegas, we came to the empty desert highway with the same nothingness mile after mile, which made it much easier to think, drive and talk all at the same time. "Who are you?" I finally asked.

"We already established that, friend. I'm Jeff."

"Very funny. You know what I mean. Tell me the truth. Who are you?"

"I hate to sound cliché, but truth is a funny thing," he said, closing his book and turning in his seat to look at me. "I've always liked the first words of Friedrich Nietzsche's *Beyond Good and Evil.* 'Supposing truth is a woman - what then?'" He paused and waited for me to respond.

I smiled at that one. What an interesting way to look at truth. "I guess we'd be fighting a losing battle to ever think we could understand truth then because no man has yet been able to understand women."

He grinned and nodded. "Exactly. When I was in third grade, my teacher told the class we couldn't subtract a bigger number from a smaller number. Did she tell us the truth?" Without waiting for a response, he continued, "Yes, in fact, she told us the absolute truth." He paused for emphasis. "The absolute truth for a third-grader."

"Okay, so you were a third-grader. But that doesn't answer my question." I thought back to *Starman* the night before and all the other movies I'd seen like that. "So, I assume you aren't an alien, and I haven't seen any wings, so I'm guessing you're not an angel. Do you have a mom and dad?"

"Didn't Buddha? Didn't Jesus?"

In shock, I turned my head quickly towards him. Did he compare himself to Buddha and Jesus? What kind of whack job did I pick up?

The jolting of the car going off the road startled me back to reality, but we were well into the sand before I got it stopped. By that time I was so angry at the way he was playing with me, I was out of the car, slammed the door, and stormed further into the desert brush, before I realized what I was doing. I stopped and tried to figure out what to do next.

All I could think to do was yell, so I yelled, raising my hands for more emphasis. "What are you saying? Are you trying to tell me you're a messiah, or a prophet, or something like that?"

Jeff was casually leaning against the car, unruffled by both the blistering sun and me yelling at him. "Yup."

"How can you say that?" I demanded, from ten or twenty yards away from him. "What nut house did you escape from?"

"You said you wanted the truth. So I told you the absolute truth..." he paused "...as much of the truth as you are able to understand. You may be able to subtract bigger numbers from smaller numbers, but we have a long ways to go before you, or any of humankind, can understand truth much past what I've told you."

He shrugged and smiled his smile so that I was suddenly tempted to smack his already bruised and swollen face. I abruptly had a lot more sympathy for Bear. I wasn't a violent man, but *man!* was I tempted to give Jeff a beating.

"We still have a few days trip ahead of us," he continued, heedless of my violent thoughts. "We'll have lots of time to talk about it more."

I tried to speak a few times, but nothing came out. I'd picked up a madman, and he was making me into a madman. Granted, he was one who could tell the future, change an angry biker into a humble man, and God only knew what else.

I gave a wordless scream to vent the frustration, anger, exasperation, and all the other feelings bottled up in me. Then I walked back to my side of the car. I turned to look at him and tried to say something else, but again, nothing came out.

Because I'd never been able to come up with enough faith to believe what churches told me I should believe, I'd given up on religion long ago. For him to compare himself to Jesus or Buddha, that was too much; it passed too many limits for me. I'd have much preferred it if he'd said he was an alien; that I could've handled.

He calmly leaned against the car with his hands on the roof and watched me.

After about five minutes, he said, "Let's get out of this sand and back on the road. It's hot, and if the police came by, it'd be hard to explain everything. With my face looking like this, you'd most likely end up in jail."

I couldn't come up with a better plan, so I got in the car, cranked the AC to full, and once he was in, I backed out and got onto the road.

A little ways down the road, I pulled over to empty the sand out of my shoes; I hated sand in them.

As I started driving again, I finally had words. "So, a messiah or prophet? Which one are you?"

He looked over at me questioningly, then shrugged. "Which one works best for you? The truth works for either one."

I resisted this urge to scream--that kind of thing is hard on your ears in a closed-up car--and replied in my calmest voice, "What would work best for me is if you were just some hitchhiker, who I shouldn't have picked up, but did. One who I'll drop off at the very next sign of civilization. Then I'll go work this blasted contract job, pay my bills, and hopefully have enough money left over to live a normal life."

"You think that would be best for you?" he asked and waited a bit, but I didn't say anything, so he continued. "That doesn't seem to fit with the questions that have been going through your mind for years. Haven't you been wondering the exact opposite? Wondering if there isn't more meaning to life than working, paying bills and living a normal life?"

I didn't know how he knew what I'd been thinking, but surprise was beyond me. I only sighed, and said, "Everybody wonders that, not just me. There're books, classes, and movies about it. Colleges do research on it. People go to church to find that answer. It's an age-old question: How does one find meaning in life?"

He nodded in agreement, "Your blog post on that was excellent, by the way. You should really think about being a writer."

I guess surprise wasn't beyond me. I looked at him questioningly. "You're *the one* who read it?"

"Yep. *And* you're about to start learning the answer," he said smiling his endless smile.

Me? Learn the answer to the age-old question which had haunted man forever? "What?" I asked him, sure I'd misunderstood. "Me? I'm nobody special. I'm just some unemployed, normal guy. I don't even like going to church. I don't even know if I believe in God. So, the concepts of Jesus or Buddha, messiah or prophet, or whatever, doesn't even register with me. Right now, you're some crazy dude who has some cool parlor tricks."

I took my eyes off the endless road, looked over at him, and was surprised I was able to meet his smile with one of my own. "Very cool ones, by the way. Maybe you have ESP or something like that. That's more believable to me."

He didn't show any signs of being offended, merely shrugged again. "Don't get hung up on definitions. I mean, what does the word 'messiah' mean to you, anyway?"

"I guess I think of Jesus. Son of God. Apostles. The cross. Things like that."

"Sure, those are good examples of one particular Messiah. But what does the word mean?"

He was right; I'd given him an example, not a definition. "I guess I don't know."

"It literally means 'the anointed one.' It was originally used to refer to kings of Israel. But my use of the word, now, gets us on a slipperier slope, because you have the idea of Jesus all mixed up with what the word 'messiah' means and what it is. And I, in no way want to challenge that."

He definitely had a point there. "But I've already told you the churches have done a great job of taking that away from me, so you aren't doing any harm."

He looked a little sad with what I said but still kept his smile. "Sorry to hear that, Stanley. Churches, when well led, are wonderful sources of comfort and companionship, as well as excellent stewards for societal good."

"For some people," I sputtered.

He let my comment go and continued, "And the meaning of 'prophet' has changed almost as much. In Jesus' time, a prophet wasn't someone who told the future, a prophet was someone who was closer to God than most people, a person who was called to help other people feel closer to God. Prophets were often frowned upon by the established church authorities, like Jesus was, because they spoke about what it *truly* meant to be a member of the church, rather than a mindless peon who followed the church's rules."

"Semantics suck," I muttered. "You never know what people really mean."

Jeff chuckled. "I know. How about this, for as far as you and I go, as far as this trip goes, let's not get hung up on semantics. If you want me to be only a guy with cool parlor tricks--very cool parlor tricks, by the way--" he grinned at me "--then that's what I am. We'll let our time together be. *What* I am isn't important."

*What I am isn't important. Yeah, right.* But I was done, kaput, finished with that topic. Messiah, prophet, new meanings, old meanings... I couldn't handle it.

I paused for a moment trying to think of something else to talk about. "So, I'm going to learn the meaning of life, huh?" *Crap, I should have brought up the weather.*

"Yup."

I was tempted to not respond and let the topic drop, but I couldn't. "Let's pretend, for the sake of argument, you are divine in some way. Why would any divine being be with me? Why not some top scholar or top scientist?"

"What makes you think I haven't already done that? We've already established I went to third grade, so one can assume I've been busy between the third grade and now. In all that time, do you think you're the only person I've talked to?" He waited for me to process this. "Besides, who did Jesus have as his disciples? He didn't take the religious leaders of the time. He didn't take the greatest philosophers of the time. He took, as apostles, the people who were ready to hear the most absolute truth that humankind was ready to hear. Once someone *knows* the truth, their minds close to anything that doesn't support what they feel they know is the truth. You're questioning what the truth is, and your mind is ready to hear the next truth humankind is ready to hear."

He was comparing me to Jesus' apostles. "We're done talking messiah-stuff."

"Okay."

We drove on, while I thought. What was I supposed to do? Was I supposed to believe he was going to teach me the meaning of life? Was I playing apostle to his messiah?

I really, really, really didn't like those words, but everything I'd learned about him showed he was an extraordinary man. Heaven knew I was inexplicably drawn to him at the stoplight, and then after that, it'd been one unexplainable event after another. I couldn't buy the 'messiah' or 'prophet' label, but he clearly wasn't 'normal' either, so what was I supposed to do?

As I thought, and he sat quietly reading, I figured the best thing to do was to ask. "So, what am I supposed to do? As much as it goes against logic and rationality, you're obviously on this trip with me for a reason and I'm not going to be able to get rid of you. So, what do you want me to do?"

He looked up from his book and shrugged his shoulders. "I don't *want* you to do anything other than be Stanley. You don't need to make anything out of this time, this time will make what it needs to make. Relax, enjoy it and see what happens. Just let yourself be Stanley."

"Somehow, I get the feeling that'll be about as easy on me as teaching Bear to not cuss was on you."

He smiled.

I didn't want to explore the issue anymore, so I didn't say anything either, and we drove on.

* * *

The topography started to change and soon we were entering the Virgin River Gorge. It's a spectacular drive with the highway cut through the mountains showing the uplifted strata towering over the highway. I was glad we weren't talking right now because I'd always enjoyed this part of the drive on the trips the family and I have taken to the Rockies.

As we were leaving the gorge, my passenger asked, "Do you mind stopping up here at St. George? This town has one of my favorite bookstores. You can find almost anything there. And they have great prices."

The last sentence made me laugh. "I watched you pay a hundred bucks for one book, two thousand for another book, and now you're telling me you're a bargain shopper?"

He smiled, or kept smiling.

The idea of stopping at the bookstore sounded like a nice break so I willingly took the exit. He directed me through the town and to the bookstore. I parked and we went in.

I loved the place instantly. Right as we walked in was a large seating area with couches, recliners and books scattered about on end tables, coffee tables and small shelves. A man reached up and adjusted the lamp near the chair he was reclined in as relaxed as he would have been in his own living room. That's what the area seemed like, an oversized living room with people sitting and reading. Past that area, the real bookstore started with high wooden shelves creating a maze instead of an orderly pattern. Right away the arrangement called me in to explore.

Jeff turned left towards a U-shaped counter formed from an antique soda fountain. Both to the left and right of the counter were chairs and tables to match the soda fountain's era. Refrigerated glass display cases filled with pastries, sandwiches and other food, filled in both sides of the U. The number of people in the eating area, opposite the counter from us, made the atmosphere feel alive. It wasn't a library atmosphere at all.

Jeff placed his hands on the counter and leaned in as he watched an elderly man with his back to us hand a plate with a piece of pie on it over the display case to a customer. The elderly man wiped his hands on his apron as he turned. His face rose to meet with Jeff's and lit up. With effort, he walked around to the opening of the U, where Jeff met him, and gave Jeff a hug.

The man then stepped back to give Jeff's abused face a better look. With a very gentle and kind voice he said, "Oh, Jeff! What did you go and do?"

Jeff looked excited to see the man, put his arm around the old man's shoulders and pulled him in close. "It's not as bad as it looks. I was just helping someone out of a mess. But it's great to see you, George." After they hugged again, Jeff led the man to me. "I'd like you to meet my friend, Stanley."

George shook my hand with great eagerness and gave me a hug, also.

"George," Jeff said when the old man released me, "I can't stay too long today. I need to pick up a few books and then Stanley and I have an appointment to keep."

An appointment was news to me.

Jeff walked off and disappeared down a book-filled maze.

Looking over at George, with his thick glasses and stooped back, I thought, *this man knows Jeff.* I wanted to stick around and get some questions answered. "So, you and Jeff know each other?"

George turned his attention to me and smiled. "Oh, yes indeed. He has been coming in here for years. His parents started bringing him here when he was a little tyke."

Gold mine! "You knew his parents?"

"Oh, yes. Extremely pleasant people. And actually, I should have said, Jeff had been bringing his parents here since he was a little boy. They simply got some desserts and patiently talked as their little boy ran from bookshelf to bookshelf; searching for books he hadn't read."

"He used to live around here?"

"Oh, no. From Pennsylvania somewhere. He just liked this store for some reason." He paused and looked around the store with a smile full of pride. "Actually, for a very good reason; I love this place. He liked coming here, so his parents brought him a couple times a year."

George walked over to the antique soda fountain and started filling a glass as he continued. "Over the years, it's gotten harder for him to find books he hasn't read. He's read most of them in here."

I'd followed him and sat in one of the stools along the soda fountain.

He handed the glass to me as he kept talking, not even asking whether I wanted the drink or not. "He buys them, reads them, and then brings them back. Won't take any money when he brings them back, either. I'll bet he's bought some of the books on these shelves three or four times."

George was an easy guy to listen to. As I raised the glass to my mouth, the smell of root beer filled my nose. I took a drink and was rewarded with the creamiest root beer I'd ever tasted.

George noted my reaction with a smile and continued telling me about Jeff. "He has me keep multiple copies of some books in stock. Those, he never brings back. I keep restocking them and he buys more." George paused for a while in reflection. "His parents, such a nice couple; one of the nicest couples you'd ever wish to meet. But I don't think they knew quite what to think of their son, any more than you or I do."

Jeff suddenly appeared, startling me.

"Got what I needed, George. Sorry, we can't stay longer."

George took the glass right out of my hand, and I wanted to protest because I'd only had two drinks from it and was thoroughly enjoying it. But to my relief, he poured my drink into a to-go cup, filled another one for Jeff and handed them to us.

George rang up the books and, without even looking at the total, Jeff laid a hundred-dollar bill on the counter. George took it saying with mild annoyance, "Yes, yes, yes, I know. Either a tip or pay for the next people in line." It was clear George had been through this with Jeff over many years. Then George made his way around the counter and hugged Jeff and me. He held Jeff's arms as he examined the battered face. "Be safe, my good friend. Come back soon and stay longer."

Jeff looked lovingly at the old man. "I'll try to get back soon." He turned and I followed him out.

So much for my gold mine of information, I thought as I got back into the car. But it was worth the stop for the glass of root beer itself. What a wonderful place.

# Chapter 9

As we got back onto the highway, I inquired of Jeff, "So, what appointment do we have?"

Jeff looked at the time on the dash and said, "We have a couple hours to get there, but I promise it won't ruin your time schedule too bad. You'll get to your job on time."

I was already a day behind, but I still had Sunday to rest once I got there, so I wasn't too worried. "That doesn't answer my question."

He looked over at me. "What was the question again?"

A bit exasperated I huffed, "What appointment do we have?"

He tilted his head back in understanding. "Ah, the appointment. Yes. Too hard to explain right now. Don't worry, you'll know soon enough."

I started to protest but I knew Jeff was putting me off, so I let it drop.

We drove until Jeff told me to get off on the exit for Zion National Park. He guided me down some picturesque park roads until we got to a parking lot by a scenic overlook, and Jeff told me to park. After I did so, we got out.

He reached into the back and dragged up the bag from George's store. He looked through the books, stuck one in his back pocket, and held another out one to me.

As I walked around the car to take it, he said, "This is a great reading spot. There's a cliff overlooking the river. It's a breathtaking view. Very peaceful. It shows all God's glory. Come on, we don't want to be late."

Late? Like the cliff and river wouldn't be there if we didn't get there in time? And it was too early to be rushing for the sunset.

Mystified, I matched his hurried pace as we followed a trail to the top of the cliff. I looked out over the view and he was right; it was magnificent. He jumped the guardrail and continued down a rarely used trail. With a shrug, I followed.

We came to an overhang under where we had been standing a little bit ago. He went to the back wall of the cliff's face, pulled the book out of his back pocket and sat down.

Was this the appointment we had? To sit under a cliff and read? Confused, I sat beside him and looked at the book he'd handed me. *Flatland, A Romance of Many Dimensions,* by Edwin Abbott Abbott. I opened the cover and looked at the publication date, 1884. Guess Jeff isn't into modern literature, I thought with a smile.

I started reading, and as I did, I began to understand why Jeff liked this spot. The wind made an interesting sound as it passed through the cliffs and the color of the rocks gave the air a red tint.

We'd been sitting there only a few minutes when I heard someone coming down the trail.

The person walked in front of us, but faced out to the river and stood at the cliff's edge, looking out.

Jeff and I watched him for a minute. I could tell it was a high school kid because he had a high school's football team T-shirt on, which looked familiar, but he was angled wrong so I couldn't make out the city's name on it. We watched him for a few minutes, and I thought about that T-shirt. Where had I seen it before?

Then I saw the boy's legs and body tense. *Crap!* He's going to jump!

"Fancy meeting you here, friend," Jeff announced calmly.

That startled the young man so much he almost fell forward, but after a pulse-pounding moment, he caught his balance and quickly turned around to face us.

The breath I was about to suck in got stuck in my throat as I choked in recognition. I don't know why I keep being shocked, but I stared in disbelief as it became clear where I'd seen that T-shirt. Harris, the student who sold the book to Jeff in Sally's restaurant, stared back at us in disbelief.

Jeff stood, tucked the book in his back pocket, and slowly walked towards the kid.

I wasn't sure if he recognized Jeff with his lambasted face, but Harris's stupefied expression showed his unease.

As Jeff got closer, he calmly said, "Isn't this a great place, Harris? My parents used to bring me here when I was very young."

At the edge of the cliff, Jeff paused a comfortable distance away from Harris, and they both looked out at the spectacular vista until Harris finally spoke.

"My parents would bring me and my brother and sister here too before they …" He stopped. "I still like coming here when I need to think. Not sure why."

"It's a great place for thinking. I still come here for that." Jeff seemed to be having his own deep thoughts. "This place brings back some great memories from before my mom died."

Harris' head quickly turned to Jeff. I knew what the rest of Harris' sentence was now. They died. I just hoped the "they" wasn't his whole family.

Jeff continued, taking no notice of Harris' reaction. "It's my favorite place to remember her." Jeff paused as he thought more.

I couldn't see Jeff's face, but I could tell from the change in his tone the next words came harder.

"My dad changed after she died. I don't think he knew how to be happy without her. I wasn't sure I could be happy without her, either."

The depth of the pain in his voice surprised me. I'd only known him a short time, but in that time, he'd been in total control. A control like I'd never seen before.

Jeff continued in a way that drew me into the depths of his pain. "After she died, it was horrible. My father never fully recovered. He died a couple years later, right after I turned eighteen. I think he died from a broken heart. They were very wealthy and left me everything, but I didn't care about the money. In fact, I gave it all away and I spent the next eight years traveling, looking for answers. I found out answers for questions like I had are very hard to come by."

Harris looked at Jeff intently, but again, uncharacteristically for

Jeff, he was staring out over the cliff deep in his own thoughts.

"Tell me about it," Harris muttered.

Jeff continued his painful story. "I felt abandoned, alone. All I had left was our family butler who was like a second father to me." He now turned to Harris. "When dad died, I turned around, gave him all the money, then walked out on him for eight years. How selfish was that? I mean, I wasn't the only one who had deeply loved my parents. I wasn't the only one affected by their death. I'm sure he could have used me during that time. I'm lucky I didn't have any siblings who needed me. If I had, would I have abandoned them, too? I don't know."

Harris's expression changed to one of shame mixed with deep sadness.

Watching Jeff was magical. I could tell the words he used were not random. Like with Bear, Jeff's words meant something deep to Harris, and I could see Harris react to them.

After a minute or two of Harris silently looking at Jeff, Jeff gently placed his hand on Harris' shoulder. At the touch, Harris broke down and fell into Jeff's arms, crying.

Jeff held Harris until he calmed.

After a few long minutes, Harris pulled away and embarrassedly swiped at the tears on his face. "Sorry 'bout that."

"No problem," Jeff replied with his gentle smile. "Have faith it will be fine and use what goes wrong to get the energy to do what is right."

Harris gave a hint of a smile. "They need me. My little brother and sister." He looked at Jeff thankfully. "They need me."

Jeff nodded and turned him away from the edge of the cliff and patted him companionably on the back. "You need a ride back?"

"Nah," answered Harris. "I can make it."

"Good." As he walked, Jeff turned to me. "Let's get back on the road, Stanley."

When I got up and brushed the dirt from my behind, Harris gave me a weird look, like he'd forgotten I was there. Which didn't surprise me. I'd already discovered that when Jeff turned his attention on you, the rest of the world disappeared. So, I didn't take it personally.

We headed up the hill, them in front chatting softly, and I followed, deep in my own thoughts.

When we got to the cars, Jeff took the book out of his back pocket and opened it. I peeked at the title: *Man's Search for Meaning* by Viktor Frankl. As usual, Jeff wrote in the front cover and handed it to Harris.

"Would you read this for me, friend?" he asked the boy. "I think it'll help you through this tough time."

Harris looked at the book Jeff held out and hesitantly reached out and took it. "Yeah, I guess."

Jeff gave him one of his patented smiles and a friendly pat on the back as we turned toward Harris' car. "Call me after you finish it or call me if you need to talk. Anytime. The number's in the front of the book."

I knew whose number he'd written.

The boy stood by his car for a few minutes, looking Jeff in the eye. I don't know what silent communication passed between them, but whatever it was, seemed to lift a huge weight off Harris' shoulders. He gave Jeff a shaky smile, and surprisingly, a hug, then got in his car and drove off.

\* \* \*

Without any words between us, Jeff and I got into the Jetta, and we started back down the park roads to the highway.

"So, that's why you looked at the boy so strangely at the restaurant?" I asked once I'd finally gotten back up to highway speed.

Jeff nodded while he stared out the front window.

"And he said he needed the money. You knew he was going to use it to buy gas to come kill himself?"

Again, Jeff nodded as he stared forward.

It was so unlike him and I started to realize how deeply affected he was by the encounter with Harris. This made me think of my parents. I take them for granted like they will always be around and there for me. I made a mental note that Beth, the kids and I need to go see them more.

"Sorry about your parents, Jeff."

He nodded in acknowledgment. "Thanks. It was hard, but it's what needed to happen to make me who I am today."

I looked at him not knowing how to respond. My first reaction was to say "it's all part of the experience," but I'm glad I filtered myself because that sounded cold.

Before I could come up with anything else, Jeff turned to me. "Enough of the depressing stuff." Then he smiled. "Let's see what your taste in music is like." He grabbed my CD collection from behind my seat and started going through them.

As he did, I slowed down for two cars driving side-by-side on the mostly empty expressway, going ten miles-an-hour under the speed limit. I pulled into the left lane, hoping that car was going faster than the other, but it wasn't. As there wasn't anywhere else for me to go, and nothing for me to do until somebody decided to speed up or slow down so I could get between them, I had time to sputter to myself and look at the car's collection of bumper-stickers.

I usually found them amusing, because they often said so much about the owners of the cars. But right now, the "WWJD" sticker on the left-lane car only annoyed me more.

"What would Jesus do?" I mumbled to myself. I'm pretty sure Jesus wouldn't cruise in the left lane pacing the car in the right when it was obvious I wanted to pass!

Beth's church had gotten hung up on the whole WWJD bandwagon a while back, which annoyed me. I kept thinking one thing Jesus wouldn't do is get caught up in some stupid slogan. He'd live like he was telling others to and not put a rubber wristband or T-shirt on, to try to make people think he was something he wasn't.

A quick flash of guilt hit me as I mentally chided myself for being so cynical. I'm sure the WWJD idea had started with the best of intentions, and I'm sure there were people out there who truly did live Jesus' message, but I sure hadn't seen nearly as many of those people as I had the posers or hypocrites.

Looking over at the guy with the messiah-complex going through my CD collection, I had to chuckle. This should be interesting I thought, WWJLT, What Would Jesus Listen To?

Right as I thought that, Jeff held out a CD and triumphantly exclaimed, "The Ramones! Great! These guys were never impeded by thought." He pushed the CD in the player, and my brain took a much-needed rest and after the left lane car slowed down enough I moved to the right, squeezed between them, and we were able to continue down the road.

# Chapter 10

An hour or so later we turned onto I-70 and headed towards the Rockies. I've always loved the Rockies and was looking forward to driving through them. I figured we could stop for the night before we got far into them so I could do the pretty drive in the light. It would add time to the rest of the trip, but I wanted to enjoy this part.

We made good time and drove until my stomach was letting me know it was dinnertime. Between eating lunch and snacking, we'd finished most of the sandwiches Beth had made, which meant we needed restaurant food. But when I thought about stopping, I got nervous. So far, every time we'd stopped bizarre things had happened, and I didn't need any more of that, which was exactly why somebody had invented the drive-thru.

"I'm getting hungry," I announced, "but we need to make up some time. You okay with going through a drive-thru?"

Jeff looked at me with a joking look in his smile. "Are you trying to keep me away from people, Stanley?"

"Do you want the truth?" I asked, smiling back.

"I'm not sure I could handle it, so a drive-thru it is. You pick one. I'm okay with anything."

The knots in my stomach loosened up.

We pulled into a fast food place just off the highway, got some burgers, fries, and malts, and were on the road again. As more miles flowed under the wheels, things were almost normal. He read while we listened to some more music, the mountains grew closer and the sun began to set. He had good taste in music.

I still didn't know what to make of Jeff and questions to ask him were continually running through my mind. He was, obviously, not your normal sort of guy. But a messiah or prophet? That was too far out for me.

Of all the people in the world, why would *I* be on a road trip with a twenty-first-century messiah? God only knew--realizing the next part of that thought, I chuckled to myself at my joke--I questioned the existence of God. *God also knows how funny I am.* But rationalizing the first-century messiah was too much for me, let alone a twenty-first-century one.

So, what else could he be? Or maybe he had ESP? I'd never experienced anybody with ESP, so much like my lack of belief in the existence of God, I had no grounds to believe in any paranormal explanation.

What did that leave me?

At which point, my over-saturated science-fiction imagination kicked in and brought me back to the alien theory. But that seemed even more far-out than a twenty-first-century messiah, so I backed up a couple steps and replayed what I'd actually experienced with him.

Unable to wrap my brain around it, I began to wonder what life must be like for him. "So, you can tell the future and read minds, does that complicate or simplify things?"

He looked at me thoughtfully as he adjusted his seat belt and turned towards me a little. "Good question. Simplify? No. Definitely not. Complicate? Knowing what I know doesn't make it complicated, but can definitely take all the fun out of life. Especially since I love surprises. So, for the most part, I shut it down as best I can, and live as a normal human being."

I looked at him skeptically.

He smiled and continued. "As normal as I can. For example, the bar-thing yesterday was your doing. I was letting things go to see where they went. It was a lot of fun." Rubbing his battered face, he added, "Really, really painful, but fun."

I was trying to pay attention to him and still watch the road. The semi in front of me had slowed, so I put on my blinker, checked my mirrors and moved to the left lane.

Jeff waited for me to get back in the right lane, then said, "You were right about Harris in the restaurant. That is partly why I was taken aback by him. I knew we'd be seeing him again. But the other reason was because I'm bothered by how many humans have such a lack of interest in learning and growing."

Him using the word 'humans' made me lean more towards my alien theory. It was like he was separating himself from us.

"Even if Harris hadn't been anticipating his drive to that cliff, he'd have sold me that book, not realizing what a treasure he'd given away." Jeff was thoughtful for a moment and then got an amused look on his face. "We fixed both things today. He'll recover. The hole in his life from his parents' death will always be there, but that hole will push him into greatness. He'll read most of that book tonight. Doubt if he even sleeps. When he gets to school tomorrow, his teachers will wonder who he is, because the same body will hold a different man."

Two things crossed my mind. One, he said *we* fixed that tonight, but I didn't do anything. Two, I was reminded of Bear's Saul-to-Paul conversion, and I was in awe of Jeff's ability to say exactly what needed to be said in both situations. It was amazing how fast he could change somebody so dramatically. After seeing Bear change, I expected Harris's change to be as profound. "Yeah, I'll bet you're right."

We fell back into silence. And again, as the miles rolled, so did my questions, as I tried to comprehend Jeff, who he was, what I'd seen him do, what he had said.

Spending so many years in a church with an irrational belief system had done serious damage to my already shaky Christian roots. So, to be sitting here with a guy who claimed to be a messiah or prophet wasn't making any sense to me.

My rational half was saying he was nuts and to drop him off right now. But after everything I'd seen in the last two days, *I* had to admit absolutely nothing supported me not accepting him for what he said he was, other than my own lack of faith.

After more miles and more questions, my rational half decided I had three choices. One, Jeff was a liar. Two, he was a nut. Or three, he was telling the truth.

The first two didn't fit with what I'd seen of him. But no matter how hard I tried, I couldn't make the last one fit either, no matter which way I looked at it.

I was at a complete loss for what to believe. So, in some ways, nothing had changed with me. I felt the same way every Sunday after church.

Looking over at him, reading yet another book, I studied his face as well as I could while staying between the lines of the road. I'm not sure what a madman or a liar should look like, but it didn't seem like I was seeing it buckled into the seat beside me.

So, again, a logical person would cautiously assume he was what he said he was until evidence supported otherwise.

Nope, that still wasn't working for me. As far as I knew, there might not even be a God, much less a human manifestation of God on Earth.

Before I realized what I was saying, I blurted out, "According to the church, Jesus came to save us from our sins, so if you're a prophet or messiah or whatever, why are *you* here?"

He unhurriedly looked over at me with a calm face. After a longish pause, apparently to gather his thoughts, he replied, "In essence, to update an ancient message for modern people."

I glanced at him questioningly.

"When Jesus walked the Earth, human's technical abilities were slowly advancing, and religion guided their lives, playing a much larger role in their lives than reason."

"Yeah," I said. I'd done a fair amount of research in my quest to understand Beth's church.

"Jesus came and told them the truth--that all is love--in a way they were able to understand, two thousand years ago."

"Okay, I get that." And it made sense, even though I'd never put it in quite those terms. "But--" I prompted.

"Things are much different now," he continued with his never-ending smile. "In fact, it's almost the opposite. Humans' technology is advancing very quickly, but religion is typically a very small part of everyday life. Reason, right or wrong, now guides most people's lives."

I made a disagreeing sound, as I knew plenty of people who didn't have even a nodding acquaintance with reason. But I got his point and motioned him to keep going.

"The message humans need to hear now is basically the same, but the way it's told has to be different than when Jesus was here. It has to be told in a way that matches how humans have grown and changed. And because humans have grown, they are ready for *more* of the message, a broader message, than the people of Jesus' time. Humans are ready to learn to subtract bigger numbers from smaller numbers," he concluded, referring back to his third-grade-math metaphor.

He let me think as I looked out the windshield and slowed for the car I was approaching. The nice thing about driving is I have a reason not to make eye contact.

He had an interesting point, but it didn't fully work in my mind. "I'm not sure humans have advanced that much."

I got into the left lane to pass the car, then continued, "I look around at this world and wonder if there is any reasoning going on at all. Our politicians are more interested in supporting their party, getting re-elected or stopping the opposing party than in doing the right thing. And there are plenty of churches more interested in how full their donations plates are than truth." I thought about a couple of the mega-church services I'd accidentally caught, before the cable was shut off, with all their fancy productions and very little substance in their sermons. "Their services are designed to entertain, not enlighten. Reason seems to play a small part in how today's world works."

"You are *so* right about that," Jeff replied. "Many topics are so highly polarized, neither side is even close to right, and neither side is even worried about being right, they're only interested in winning a fight that doesn't even need to be fought. Taking sides on a topic that doesn't need sides. And then there are the people who make careers and lots of money by polarizing topics even more. Even sadder is the number of people who'll support someone whose main purpose in life is of no value other than the polarization of ideas. I didn't say humans are actually subtracting big numbers from small numbers, but they're ready to learn how to do so. There's some growing that still needs to happen but the pieces are in place."

I snorted. "There's a lot of growing that needs to happen."

"Not really. The gap is pretty small and can be closed quickly. Once the focus starts to change, everything will be different."

I realized I needed to change my focus. I was cruising in the left lane while I listened to him. I put my blinker on and changed back to the right lane. After I finished, I asked, "The focus needs to change from what to what?"

"That's not a one sentence or one day answer. We can start it today, but we'll only start to touch on it. If I asked you what needed to change, what is the first thing that comes to your mind?"

That was easy. It was the thing that caused me most of my anxiety most of my life. "Money."

"Great. That's an easy place to start. So, let's say the focus needs to shift from money."

The images of Jeff passing out hundred-dollar bills played through my mind. "But that isn't going to mean much coming from you. You obviously don't have any money problems."

"If you had all the money you needed, would your life be better, Stanley?" Jeff asked with a penetrating look.

I answered with a huff, "It'd sure beat struggling my whole life to get by. I've been out of work for five months." My voice rose. "My wife and I are barely keeping the house from being foreclosed on. Our credit cards are maxed out. We've taken the kids out of everything because we can't pay for it. In five months of searching, the only thing I've been able to get is this two-month contract job, and it's clear across the country from my family, but I have to take it because if I don't, we won't even be able to keep the lights on. And this month, we aren't paying the mortgage, so I'd have enough for gas and food for the trip, but I can't afford to pay for hotels! So, sure! All the money I needed would be way better than this!" I didn't realize I was crying until I finished. I guess all I'd seen with Jeff and all the money stress from being out of work had built up.

Jeff didn't say anything, and I tried to calm down. For a distraction I glanced at the gas gauge and decided this was a good time to get gas. "Speaking of gas, we need to stop."

"Let's get some road trip snacks too," Jeff said in a tone obviously meant to cheer me up. "Nothing makes a trip better than buying overpriced nutritionally void," he did the air quotes, "food." *Like food was going to help*. But instead of saying anything, I took the next exit, looked at the gas price signs and found the station with the cheapest diesel. I pulled up to the pump and we got out. I took my credit card out of my wallet and started to stick it into the pump, but Jeff called out, "Did you forget who's buying the gas, Stanley?"

I stopped and looked over towards him.

"Hey, with me on this trip, maybe you can pay your mortgage. But I only have cash so we have to go in and prepay."

I looked at him for a long moment. I didn't like feeling like I was taking charity, then shrugged. I was giving him a ride; he could pay for the gas. "Works for me."

We started heading into the convenience store. "It makes me mad," Jeff said as he opened the door for us, "I have to prepay. Now I have to make two trips and stand in line twice."

That sounded odd coming from a man who claimed to be the messiah.

*Whoa!* Where did that thought come from? I stopped in the chips aisle. Had Jeff actually *claimed* to be the messiah? I know he'd compared himself to Jesus and Buddha, but I didn't recall him saying he was. I replayed the conversation again. He'd said I could pick which words worked best for me, but hadn't actually said he was either, or maybe he did, I couldn't remember.

But regardless, it seemed strange for him to be upset about having to prepay.

He continued as he grabbed a couple bags of chips, "I understand why they do it because of all the drive-offs. It gets back to what I was saying about humans advancing in knowledge but not spiritually." He headed back to the coolers. "Spiritually void people feel the world owes them something and taking gas without paying for it is part of what they feel is owed to them."

"Personally, I'd never thought of getting gas as a spiritual experience," I said trying to lighten my mood.

He started laughing so hard I thought the veins in his head were going to burst, which didn't go well with all the cuts and bruises. It was a busy place and people were turning and looking at us.

"Oh, friend, I didn't see that coming. That made my day," he said as he tried to get his laughter under control. "You know, when I told you earlier, I turn it off most of the time? This is why. If I knew what you were going to say it wouldn't be funny. It'd be like knowing the punch lines of every joke. Life is one punch line after another," he paused and felt his face, "and some very hard punches." He burst out laughing again.

Everybody in the store was looking at us, and I debated pretending I didn't know him as we stood in the cooler aisle with him until he gained his composure.

Still chuckling occasionally, he finished his circuit of the store, picking up his nutritionally void 'food' and drinks. "Anything particular you want?"

I shook my head no. He had the Mt. Dew, and all the other stuff seemed right for road trip snacks. So, I followed as he got in line.

When we finally got to the cashier, he put the stuff on the counter, then pointed to the display of lottery tickets and asked the clerk, "Which scratch-off has the highest prize?"

"Number seven has a $250,000 top prize," the clerk answered in a why-do-people-keep-asking-me-that voice.

"I'll take one of those, and I'm filling up on pump number seven. I need a bag of ice, too." He handed the clerk a hundred-dollar bill, which he must have an infinite stream of. He then glanced back at the people in line and handed the clerk another hundred-dollar bill. "I don't want to come back in for the change," he quietly said. "Use this for the people behind me for as long as it will go. Don't tell them it was me, though."

The clerk lost his this-is-a-stupid-job look, cocked his head a little and took the money. "You sure, mister? That's a lot of money?"

Jeff nodded.

The clerk shrugged. "Whatever." He put all Jeff's road trip food in a bag, handed the scratch-off to Jeff and we walked out and got the ice.

As we walked to the Jetta, he handed me the lottery ticket.

I stared at him blankly as I took it.

Jeff started to pump the gas, and I stood beside the car with the ticket in one hand and took a coin out of my pocket with the other. My mind was numb. I started to sweat. Everything around me stopped as my mind replayed all the different scenes where Jeff had shown his extraordinary abilities. Then it replayed the conversation right before we pulled in: "If you had all the money you needed, would your life be better, Stanley?"

After what seemed like an eternity, I rested the ticket on the top of the car, raised the coin to the ticket, scratched off one box, moved to the next--my heart beating faster with each box--and then the last one. In disbelief, I stared at the card, then ran to the trash can and threw up.

# Chapter 11

As I was leaning over the trash, emptying a lifetime of stress, Jeff walked up and took the ticket out of my hand and looked at it. With a total disregard for my distress, he exclaimed, "Hey! You won ten bucks. You did better than I ever do. I don't know why I even buy them. Can we cash it in next time we stop? I don't want to stand in line, again."

Finally, ending my relationship with the trash can, I grabbed a window cleaning paper towel from the dispenser on the post, wiped my face, then got the car keys out of my pocket and tossed them to Jeff. I opened the passenger door, reached around the seat, and shoved everything out from behind the seat, and reclined it as far as it could go. I then grabbed my pillow, leaned it against the door, shoved my face into it, and shut my eyes.

I heard the driver-side door shut and the engine start.

The next thing I knew, Jeff was gently shaking me and handing me a room key. I blearily looked around and saw he'd taken my stuff out of the car and was pointing toward a room. I walked in, shut the door, pulled back the covers, took off my shoes, and curled up in the bed.

\* \* \*

I woke up, groggily looked at my phone, three o'clock, Friday morning, about seven hours after my incident with the trash can. I debated trying to go back to sleep, but my head was pounding. Wishing desperately for some pain killers, but having none, I did my best to ignore it. After I brushed my teeth, for obvious reasons,

I figured I was too wide awake to go back to sleep, so I went ahead and took a shower.

After the shower, I turned on the TV and was disappointed they didn't have a Sci-Fi channel. It's hard enough to find something worth watching during primetime, at three in the morning it's next to impossible. I shut it off.

Jeff had brought some of the snacks into my room and the cooler with drinks. I flopped in the chair, opened a bag of chips, and grabbed a handful.

Seeing my phone beside the bag, reminded me I hadn't called Beth last night like I said I would. After telling her about the strange trip yesterday and not calling her today, I was tempted to call her right then. But when I checked my phone, I hadn't missed any calls or text messages, so I figured she wasn't worried and I could wait until a better time to call.

The book Jeff gave me yesterday was sitting with the rest of the stuff, so I picked it up and looked at it. *Flatland: A Romance of Many Dimensions*, written almost a hundred and thirty years ago.

As I opened it to read some more of the introduction, which I'd started on Harris' cliff face, I realized this wasn't a random book like I'd seen him give Sally and Bear. Jeff had gone to the bookstore and bought it specifically for me. I wondered if this was one of the books George kept stocked for Jeff; one of the books that never makes it back to the store.

I started reading and was quickly enthralled until my phone rang scaring the crap out of me and setting my head to pounding again. But thankfully, after a moment it settled back down to irritating background noise.

I glanced at the clock as I reached for the phone; it was a few minutes after 7AM. I was both glad and nervous when I saw it was Beth. We crossed a time zone soon after Las Vegas so it was 6AM her time. She was up early for a reason and that reason might be me. I answered hesitantly. "Good morning, Beth," I said as I readied myself for what was to follow.

She answered in a calm voice, but her too sweet tone let me know I'd screwed up again. "Good morning, Stanley. Did you forget something last night?"

My first reaction was to say something like, "No, I brushed my teeth," but I fought off the urge. I've found out the hard way, I'm actually not that funny. "Sorry, but I have a good reason." I paused to rethink that reason. "Well, maybe not a good reason but an interesting one."

"I'm listening," she said, with more concern than I felt comfortable with.

I started off, interested myself to see how the story went. "In the morning, I was going to take off without him. I had everything ready to go until I started looking for my keys."

Beth sighed.

"But the good news is he filled up the car before I even got up," I said trying to redeem myself.

"Stanley," she said with that wife voice which lets you know how much you messed up.

I tried to think of what to say to make it alright. "Don't worry, Beth. He's really a nice guy." I then tried to come up with supporting evidence and the scene from the cliff popped into my head. "He even stopped this high school kid from killing himself."

"What?"

I told her about the trip to Zion, and how Jeff knew the kid was going to be there, but as soon as I said the words, I realized this wasn't the direction I wanted to go, but now was too late.

"So Jeff knew?" She wasn't sounding convinced.

"Well, yeah, he did." This sounded bad, even to me. "The day before yesterday, he had me stop at a *green* light right before a motorcycle ran its red light. The motorcycle would've hit me right in my door if Jeff hadn't stopped me. And this morning at breakfast, he told me exactly what was going to happen, and it happened."

The sarcasm was thick as she said, "So, you're on the road with a fortune-teller? I'm feeling so much better now, Stanley. Thanks for the peace of mind."

"I don't know what to tell you, Beth!" I said with a lot of emotion but not yelling. I almost told her about driving off the road after the messiah vs. prophet conversation but that wouldn't have helped. "There's really, really something about him. It's like

I'm supposed to be on this trip with him. Everything feels like that. It's all strange and stressful, yet, he's here to teach me something."

"Stanley," was her response in a worried voice.

"I mean it. Oh, get this. Last I checked, my blog post had one view. Want to guess who read it?"

"Really?"

"Yeah. How strange is that? I write a blog post, questioning the meaning of life, I get one view, immediately get a job offer across the country and there just happens to be a hitchhiker within miles of our house going to the exact same city on the other side of the country and that hitchhiker was the one who read my blog post." I paused and waited for her response. When it didn't come, I was about to say something else but was stopped.

"I have to admit, when you say it like that, it sounds, I don't know, but less than a coincidence. I really don't know what to think."

"Right. I don't know either but things keep happening. Like, we had this conversation about money, and I told him how hard it's been lately. He asked me if money would take care of my problems, and I said it would sure beat the situation now. Then when we stopped for gas, he bought me a lottery ticket, Beth. I'd seen this guy predict the future, multiple times in the last two days, and he handed me a lottery ticket!" I paused, thinking about that myself and replaying the event.

"I take it we didn't win, otherwise you'd have told me." She sure was a smart woman.

"Well, we kind of won. Will ten dollars help us much?"

"Ten dollars, huh?" I could visualize her shaking her head on the other end of the phone. "So, then what?"

"Then I threw up in the trash can and passed out in the car."

I was starting to feel better after telling all of this, but I don't think it was doing her any good.

"Where are you?" she asked.

That caught me off guard. I hadn't thought of that. I quickly looked at the nightstand for some information about the hotel and found it on the room's phone. "Huh. I'm in Denver," I said to myself as much as to her.

Jeff had driven all the way over the Rockies before stopping. I was annoyed, mixed with anger and happiness. He made some great distance while I was passed out, and now I wouldn't have to worry about being late for my first day, but at the same time, the part of the trip I was most looking forward to, I'd missed.

Beth didn't respond. I think she was expecting some ludicrous answer, but Denver was reasonable from her perspective.

"He got a book for me at the bookstore, yesterday, too. After I couldn't sleep this morning, I started reading. It's about a two-dimensional being, called a square, who has a dream about visiting a one-dimensional world, and then he gets a visit from a three-dimensional being, called a sphere."

In a questioning voice, Beth said, "Okay?" and then waited for me to give the significance for telling her this.

That is exactly what I was trying to do before she interrupted me with the phone call. Why did Jeff give me this book? "I don't know if it means anything, Beth. It's just an interesting choice of books for him to give me."

She waited a few seconds. "So, now what?"

I didn't see I had much choice. "I finish the trip with my strange, new friend, and see what happens."

Again, she waited. "I trust your judgment, Stanley."

"That's freaking me out, Beth. After everything I've told you, I'd have never thought I'd hear you say that."

In an exasperated voice, she said, "Bye, Stanley. Maybe I can sleep for a little bit now that I know you're okay. You'd better call me tonight. I love you."

"I'll call. Don't worry. I love you, too," and the call ended.

After I put the cell phone on the nightstand, I sat there for a while. The book he'd given me was intriguing on its own. But to read it, in light of who gave it to me, made my mind hurt thinking about my strange hitchhiker and all I'd seen him do. I'd read a lot of stuff on string-theory and M-theory, which said our universe had ten or eleven dimensions. Was this what he was telling me by giving me this book? Was he like the sphere visiting the square and trying to explain the third dimension? With my limited understanding of time as a dimension, this would explain his ability to predict the future.

Another interesting thing was the square was shocked the sphere could see his insides. From the square's two-dimensional perspective, he was a closed system. Everything he saw was merely lines, and the shapes of the other two-dimensional beings were not obvious. The sphere, from its three-dimensional vantage point, could see the exact shape of everything and see *inside* the squares. The square then asked the sphere if "the One" from the land of four-dimensions could see the insides of a being of a three-dimensional world. The sphere scoffed and said that was "utterly inconceivable." Myself--a being in the third-dimension--agreed with the sphere, it was utterly inconceivable. Yet, if there was a fourth-dimensional being, as the square hypothesized, it would seem magical to us, like it had super-powers. Or maybe even omnipotent.

My train of thought was interrupted by a knock on the door.

"Come in!" I hollered, which set my head to pounding, again. If this kept up, we'd be hitting the drugstore before breakfast, because driving like this wouldn't be any fun.

"The door's locked, friend," Jeff called through the door.

As the square to the sphere, I said, "Knock it off and get in here!"

The door opened and Jeff walked in with a big smile. "So, I take it you read the book."

I looked at him, and even though his face looked much better today, he sure didn't look any more multi-dimensional than I was. "Yeah, I read it." I looked at him for some clue as to what he expected from me, when he didn't give me any, I finally asked, "Is that what you're trying to tell me?"

He smiled. "I'm trying to give you perspective, Stanley. That's all. If you can start looking at things in a different way, you'll start to understand their nature. But we can talk on the way. For now, let's get going. I've filled up the Jetta and took it through the car wash. You can tell it's blue again."

I did want to get going, so holding off on the conversation seemed like a good idea. Besides, my head was hurting bad, and I guess because of my rough night, my anxiety level was pretty high.

"Okay. But do you have any Tylenol? My head hurts. I mean, it really hurts."

"No, I don't have any, but sit there." He walked over to me, placed a hand on each side of my head and then leaned forward and kissed my forehead.

I felt a strange sensation deep in my brain. A 'tingling' seemed the best way to describe it, but yet, that wasn't it.

Then inexplicably, my right hand raised itself, slugged him in the jaw and I jumped out of the chair, yelling, "What the hell are you doing?"

Then I stood there, looking at Jeff sprawled on the floor, feeling as astounded as he looked. I'm not sure why I'd reacted that way. I'd never hit anyone in my life. It must've been due to how anxious I was, or the extremely weird sensation in my brain, or him kissing me. Either way, my nerves were shot.

He got up off the floor, gingerly rubbing his jaw, and flopped into the chair I'd come out of, but of course, he was still smiling. "Please don't talk like that. I expect more from you. How's your head?"

I changed my focus from my guilt to my headache. It was gone! Plus, the anxiety was gone. I felt great, in fact. I wasn't sleepy or groggy, either. "Hey, it feels great!"

Jeff remained slouched in the chair. "I need to work on a better way to do that. Mud made with spit and mixed with my toes to give someone sight doesn't go over well, either."

Since I felt so much better, I cheerfully ignored that weird comment and said, "You ready to go?"

"Yeah." He stood with his usual effortless grace and then turned to me. "Do we need to do anything to the cleaning crew?"

"Nope. I had two bottles of shampoo and conditioner."

He gave a small laugh and we grabbed my stuff to take it to the car.

I was greeted at the door with some cool air; cool compared to what we'd had in Las Vegas. I looked around and a nearby bank's thermometer read seventy-two degrees. Why would anybody live in Las Vegas when they could have this kind of weather?

It looked like it was going to be a beautiful July day.

* * *

Not long after we got back on the road east, heading out of Denver, my phone rang and I took it out of the cupholder. It was a number I didn't know, so I handed it to Jeff. Same type of conversation, different book, *"Sadhana, the Realization of Life* is an awesome book. Tagore makes you think, doesn't he? It's one of the books you'll feel at some point you'll be drawn back to, to read again."

As I listened, I realized I needed to start reading some of the books he was talking about.

Even well out of Denver, the *Flatland* book was strong in my mind. The messiah- or prophet-thing still didn't sit well, but for some reason, a multi-dimensional being made some sense. The fact I was rationalizing Jeff's strangeness by having him be a multi-dimensional being, let me know how far over the edge I was, and that I watched too many sci-fi movies. Yet, I couldn't deny what I'd seen him do. "So, how does *Flatland* relate to you and your abilities?" I asked out of the blue.

But he took it with his usual equanimity and a shrug. "Everything will start making more sense as we go on. Don't spend this time together worrying about what I am. Spend it thinking about why I'm here, and what you need to learn."

I looked at the Rockies in my rear-view mirror and remembered last night. "Well, I've learned you can't pick winning lottery tickets." I shook my head slowly. "That was pretty cruel, what you did at the gas station last night."

"I wouldn't use the word 'cruel,' I'd say 'needed' and pretty funny." He chuckled. "You should've seen your face."

When I tried to imagine what I looked like, I laughed a little, too. If it hadn't happened to me, it would've been pretty darn funny.

"Okay. But why 'needed' instead of 'cruel'?" I asked. "'Money's the root of all evil,' 'money can't buy happiness,' or something like that?"

"Nothing like that." He closed his ever-present book and looked at me. "In and of itself, there's nothing wrong with money or having lots of it. Money is neutral, neither good nor bad. When used appropriately, it's nothing more than a symbol of energy and effort changing hands. I spend the effort to make something you don't want to make yourself, and you exchange your money for my effort, then I go use that money to buy something I don't want to make or do."

Huh. Interesting way to look at it, I thought.

After a minute, he went on. "When you thought you were going to win $250,000, what went through your mind?"

"I don't know. A bunch of stuff, I guess. Pay off the car, credit cards, medical bills, and fix some things around the house. Maybe I could even pay off the house. Take a trip with the family. Relax for a while. Money's been such an issue with us, for so long, it'd be nice not to worry about it."

"If you'd won, you wouldn't have needed the money from the contract job you're heading to. Would you have turned around and headed home?"

Actually, I hadn't thought that far ahead. "I guess I would have." I tried to answer the best I could, but I was still wondering why the lottery ticket stunt had been 'needed,' other than for its entertainment value.

"What else would you *not* do, if you had the money?"

"Well, I don't know. I guess I wouldn't... I don't think I would..." Unable to put my scattered thoughts into words, I asked, "Why'd you ask it like that? Isn't the question what I *would* do?"

"To use another one of the money clichés: 'Money changes everything.' So... you didn't like the previous question, therefore, let me ask your question: 'What would you *do* with the money?'"

"I already said bills and vacation. I would ..."

He stopped me. "$250,000 isn't enough, let's make it $250-million, and if you want more, I can do that. I could give you as much money as you wanted. So now, 'What would you do with the money?'"

I put some serious thought behind his question. "Okay. With that kind of money, I wouldn't bother fixing up my house; I'd buy a new one, a really nice one. I wouldn't need to pay off this car; I'd get some brand new ones. I've always liked boating, so maybe a yacht or a sailboat. I'd put the kids into a private school. I'd join the country club and work on my golf game. I would ..."

"Stop!" he interrupted. "If I gave you that kind of money, and you spent it like that, when I came to see you a couple years later, you'd be in the middle of a divorce, your kids would hate you, and you'd be one of the most miserable men I'd ever have had the misfortune to meet. So, since you're my friend, whom I deeply love, I'd never do that to you."

"Some friend," I muttered.

He ignored me. "Instead, I'd take you on a bizarre, cross-country trip and mess with your head so much you end up throwing up in a trash can in a gas station parking lot. And then, my friend," he said with more emphasis, "*and only then*, would you be on your way to understanding money and knowing what happiness actually is."

Once again, I didn't know how to respond. It was making my head hurt, but I didn't want to tell him because I was afraid he'd kiss me again. So, I turned my attention to easier thoughts, and asked hopefully, "You can really get me all the money I want?"

The messiah spat Mt. Dew all over the windshield.

# Chapter 12

As Jeff grabbed some napkins to clean up his mess, he said, "*This* is the reason you're on this trip with me. Not only are you close to being ready to understand the truth humankind needs to hear, but you crack me up."

"You need to let my wife know that. She gives me 'the wife' look when I say stuff like that."

"I've got a joke to tell you, and then I'll answer your question."

"This should be good."

"Oh, it is. There was this really old, really rich guy, who died and went to heaven. At the pearly gates, he begs St. Peter, 'Please, St. Peter, please, may I go back to Earth? Please, there's something important I need to bring with me to heaven. St. Peter, being a saint after all, finally relented and said, 'Okay, but no more than one suitcase full. People would notice if you brought more than that, and they'd want to bring stuff, too.' So, the rich man went back to Earth, filled up a suitcase with gold bars and hurried back to the pearly gates. Again, he faced St. Peter, who wanted to know what the man had thought was so important that he needed to bring it to heaven. Proudly, and sure he'd impress St. Peter with the greatness of his worldly accomplishments, the old man opened the suitcase. St. Peter looked at it, and then with a confused expression asked the man, 'You brought paving bricks?'"

It took me a moment to come up with the reference. And when I did I had to admit it was funny, but I just said, drolly, "The streets of heaven are paved with gold. Paving bricks. Very funny."

"But you get my point?"

"Yes. Which has always bugged me about a song in my wife's

church, the song keeps going on about how everybody will be rich and have mansions over every hilltop in heaven. That's not what heaven is about. I know that."

"Earthly money doesn't mean anything on Earth, either. Now, to answer your question: Yes, I could give you the money--"

I looked at him eagerly.

"--but I won't."

My shoulders slumped.

"Because, simply put, if you had money right now you'd seek pleasure with it."

"What should I be seeking?" I asked.

"Fulfillment."

I gave him an exasperated look, "Oh, it's so clear now."

Jeff grinned. "I know. It's not that easy. But it's also not that hard, nor is it a new concept. It's exactly what Jesus and Buddha and all those other guys tried to tell people over and over again, and yet people *still* seek pleasure over fulfillment."

"What does 'fulfillment' mean?" To me, it seemed like one of those words no two people defined the same way--like 'love'--so you're never sure what the other person meant when they used the word.

"That's the kicker, isn't it? Let me tell you a couple stories and see if that helps."

He settled into his seat like it was going to be a long story, but there was nothing in front of the car but trucks and cornfields, so a long story was fine.

"A bunch of years ago, I knew a kid who made it big with a huge recording contract and a couple of hit songs. He bought a huge mansion and was known for his wild parties. People treated him like a king."

"Yeah, I've heard about people like that. I'd imagine it'd be hard to not end up like that."

"The temptation is there, that's for sure. And this kid didn't know enough about himself to handle the adulation that came with stardom and money. During his parties, he'd feel great, but when the people left, and the house was quiet, he'd feel empty. Hating that feeling, he'd go looking for his next pleasure-fix."

Even though I suspected the kid was in for a bad end, I couldn't help teasing Jeff. "Were you at his drunken orgies?"

He smiled at me. "No, I wasn't. I heard the stories from him and others who were there. But his story isn't unique."

I looked from the road over to him. "You said you were rich when you were young. Were you included in the non-uniqueness?"

He laughed. "No. Sorry to disappoint you. No drunken orgies in my mansion." He looked at me to see if I had anything else to add.

I didn't, so he continued, "This guy moved from one pleasure-fix to the next, trying his best to never be alone. But like any drug, he needed bigger fixes to feel the same pleasure. When I confronted him, he told me I was nuts because he was the happiest guy in the world, how could he not be with all that money and attention?"

Jeff gave a sad sigh. "The kid was so busy partying he never had another hit song, and it wasn't long before the company terminated his contract. He spent the next couple years trying to hold on to his fame with advertising deals, business ventures of different types, and whatever else he could find, but he never learned the right lessons, and finally pulled the trigger of a gun."

I'd heard research on lottery winners showed the majority of them said life was worse after they won, and they wished they'd never won. *Sports Illustrated* looked at kids who got the massive sports contracts and found out only a handful had any money three years after their sports careers ended.

He looked out the front window thoughtfully. "People confusing pleasure with fulfillment is an age-old story. You'd think people would have learned by now, but most haven't. But," he said emphatically, "thankfully, many people have learned it. My second story is about one couple who lived it every day." He smiled at me. "They threw great parties."

I laughed under my breath a little. "I take it they weren't drunken orgies."

He smiled, shaking his head. "Much better. They had a magnificent house, the most beautiful place I've ever seen, hand-carved woodwork, exquisite murals on the walls and ceilings, inlaid floors that were more works of art than many of the paintings hanging on the walls."

"Sounds pretty."

"It was. And two or three times a year, they'd throw a huge bash, always for a local charity. They'd invite everybody who was anybody, and a lot of people who weren't.

"One of their guests' favorite fundraisers was the wine tasting. Everybody who wanted to join in the game had to bring a bottle of their favorite wine and a thousand bucks. The money went into the pot for the charity, and the wine was shared around. Their goal wasn't to get drunk; it was to enjoy the art and craftsmanship of winemaking while spending quality time with friends. The person who'd brought the favorite wine took home a trophy, which they had to bring back to the next party and give to the next winner. That was fun, but the part everyone liked best was there was also a trophy for the worst wine. That trophy the winner got to keep, and they were greatly coveted." Jeff laughed. "Those were good times. And other than no drugs and no orgies, the thing that most distinguished the couple from my previous young man was, when the party was over, and the house was quiet, they were happy to have each other. They enjoyed a burger alone at home as much as they enjoyed the big parties."

"That sounds nice."

"It was."

"They're gone?"

"For a bunch of years, now. But they started a tradition picked up by their friends, who also learned many things from that couple. And they, too, knew fulfillment was more important than money."

"So, do you know many other people like that? I sure haven't heard of any."

"I know lots of people like that."

"How do they find fulfillment?" As I asked it, I realized it was the same question I'd asked my whole life--How do I find meaning in my life?--but using different words.

"It's not something they *find* like you'd find a dime on the sidewalk. It's something they work very hard at. First off, they spend a lot of time in self-reflection and self-care. They know themselves very well and take care of themselves."

That sounded selfish to me. "But--"

"Not in a narcissistic way, because they are the furthest thing from being narcissists as possible. They do it in a self-loving way. Only when our own needs are met, can we meet the needs of others."

It reminded me of a T-shirt I'd once gotten for Beth. "'If Mom ain't happy, ain't nobody happy.'"

"Exactly! And secondly, they devote the rest of their time to making their little corner of the world a better place. If he's working at a fast-food restaurant, his goal is to ensure every customer leaves his restaurant in a better mood than when they went in. If she works at an office, she makes sure she puts out a quality product that betters the world and does her best to be a pleasure to work with and for. If the person's scope is bigger, and maybe they own a company, they do their best to make sure their employees and customers are the happiest they can be."

"And if he can't find a job?" I asked.

"Then maybe it's a sign it's time to go back to school to learn a new career, or to move to a new location where different opportunities are available. Or maybe it's a gift that was given to them, a gift of time for self-reflection. I can't say unemployment is only one thing because it could be so many things."

I latched on to the part about moving. "Okay, Mr. Fortune-teller, will this become a permanent job, and I'll be moving?"

His smile was a little secretive. "You'll have to wait and see."

"Thanks bunches."

"You're welcome. But to get back on topic. The most important thing about fulfilled people is their self-esteem isn't based on their wealth, or status, or what other people say about them."

That clicked in my head. "Self-actualized? Are you talking about Maslow's hierarchy of needs?"

"Good example. What I'm trying to get across goes past Maslow, but he'll take us far enough."

He paused as if reshuffling his thoughts. "So, let's say we have a bunch of self-actualized lottery winners. And let's say ten or twenty years after they won, we were to go see them. They may or may not still have all the money, but that wouldn't be what their life was about. If they still had the material wealth, they kept it through wisdom, and intelligent business or investment decisions which benefited not only themselves but others also. A great many people around them would be better off because the winners themselves were better off. If their material wealth was gone, they'd still be the wealthiest people around, because they'd have found other paths to fulfillment."

"That makes a lot of sense," I said wondering where I'd fall on the spectrum. I knew I wasn't anywhere near self-actualized, nor fulfilled.

Jeff left me to my thoughts as the miles rolled under my wheels, and I turned the conversation around like wheels in my head. What would me being fulfilled look like?

\* \* \*

About noon, we grabbed some lunch to-go and were back on our strange journey. I was glad the time was passing quickly because the monotony of the plains would have gotten to me. As I drove, our discussion replayed itself in my head, until I had thought about it enough to ask an intelligent question. "I was wondering about your statement about Maslow's hierarchy of needs only being part of it. What's the other part?"

Jeff loosened his seatbelt and turned to lean more against the door and face me. "Don't get me wrong, I love Maslow's theory but as with any explanation it's not the end-all.

"What I'm trying to convey goes past Maslow's most known writings and into a new area. In his research, he'd found a group of people who seemed to be living in a manner beyond his definition of self-actualized. He called them 'self-realized,' meaning people who've found fulfillment both in the material world and in the spiritual aspects of their lives. But Maslow doesn't go into many details about how a person would get from self-actualized to self-realized. A peer of Maslow's named Clare Graves put forward what has come to be called 'Spiral Dynamics'. It influenced Maslow's theory."

"Spiral Dynamics, it has a great name, so it must be a great theory."

Jeff ignored me and went on. "Paul Tillich gives us a path to follow in his essay *The Lost Dimension of Religion*, and Bruce Bawer takes the idea and expands it as a portion of his book *Stealing Jesus*, they call it vertical versus horizontal growth."

"Huh?" I asked intelligently.

"Horizontal growth means a person is only concerned with day-to-day living, caught up in making a living, having fun, and other things of a worldly nature. People may grow and learn by going to school, or working hard to become experts in their field, but it's only worldly or horizontal growth."

"Okay," I said. "I get that part of it."

"In contrast, vertical growth is when one is drawn towards the infinite, to grow in depth. Tillich says vertical growth is the state of being concerned about ones' own being and ones' relationship to the Universe. It's about passionately asking questions about the meaning of our existence and being willing to receive answers, even if the answers hurt."

I had to chuckle. "I know a lot of people who ask hard questions, but very few who actually want answers."

Jeff nodded. "It's very rare to find people open to hard answers. Even churches, who supposedly deal every day in the transcendent, sometimes deal only with horizontal issues, which are easier to talk about and understand. Unfortunately, these churches often condemn the vertical issues, the ones that bring people closer to a God of love and closer to understanding ourselves, because if people start asking hard questions, then they're less likely to follow the party line."

"Yeah, I can see that."

"And to tie Maslow and Tillich together, Maslow's self-realized people are the ones deeply focused on Tillich's vertical growth."

"So, you're saying they're different ways of saying the same thing?"

Jeff shrugged. "Am I? I'll let you decide that. But those are the kinds of questions that promote vertical growth. Preoccupation with who's going to be in the World Series promotes horizontal growth. You may put a lot of thought into the World Series, but you'll have no deeper understanding of yourself or your place in the Universe, or where your self-esteem comes from."

"Vertical versus horizontal growth, huh? Self-esteem?" They were something to think about.

He turned back in his seat facing out the windshield. "Yep, but again, it is not the end-all."

\* \* \*

Mid-afternoon, we stopped at a rest area, and I let Jeff drive while I napped. My three o'clock wake-up time had taken its toll. I woke up when Jeff stopped at a rest area on the western side of Kansas City. After a brief stroll to stretch, Jeff got back into the passenger side and took out one of his endless supply of books.

As I pulled out of the rest area, my stomach was letting me know it was close to dinner time. "Dinner in Kansas City all right?"

"Sure." Then added, "We'll need gas about then too."

After I got onto the highway and set the cruise control, my thoughts returned to our conversation. Self-esteem. It was an interesting thing to think about, where does it come from? I tried to recall times in my life where my self-esteem had been high and what caused it.

Recently, with the extra time on my hands, I'd taken part in a Habitat for Humanity project. I felt good after that, so I could say my self-esteem was high. But as I thought, a quote popped into my head which had always bugged me.

As I contemplated it more, I decided Jeff was the guy to ask. "Let me throw out another cliché, 'There is no such thing as a selfless act.' It's always struck me wrong, but I don't know why."

Jeff looked up from his book. "Excellent vertical-growth question." He closed his book. "As with any cliché, there's a grain of truth to it, or it wouldn't be a cliché. The same as every species on the planet scientists have figured out how to test, humans are hardwired to be altruistic, to help others."

I looked at him, confused.

"Obviously, how a person is raised, and societal and cultural issues greatly inhibit altruism, but given loving parenting and loving, accepting societies and religions, people are hardwired to be selfless. There's a built-in biological mechanism that lights up the brain's reward centers when a person performs an altruistic act. So, they get a feeling-good payback for performing the act, hence the cliché, the act isn't selfless because they like feeling good about themselves."

"Yeah. People donate to charity so they can feel better about themselves."

"Exactly. But, of course, nothing is black and white and 'selfless acts' like so many things are on a continuum. And as with any continuum, there are extremes. Some people perform acts that are so selfless that to call them anything but truly selfless-acts is nit-picky." He grinned. "Any parent who's raised teenagers knows what I mean."

I had to laugh. "So I've heard, and I'm in no hurry to find out. Although the desire to avoid jail for killing your offspring might take some of the selflessness out of the act."

"Maybe," he replied with a chuckle, but he wasn't agreeing with me. Had the guy raised teenagers, I wondered. He looked to be in his middle or late thirties, like me, so I guess it was possible.

"On the other end of the continuum is the person who does good things only for the sake of purely selfish reasons."

I mulled that over for a minute to try and come up with an example. "That would be the rich guy who gives to charities only for the sake of the promotional value of his name on a plaque and the tax write-off?"

"Yeah. Now, if you want to take your vertical growth to the next level, you ask the 'why?' question. 'Why do people perform selfless acts?'"

"You just said, biology."

"Given the parenting most people are raised with, and the racial divides that still permeate our society, and the divisiveness of many of our religions--'it's okay to look down upon your neighbor because he goes to the wrong church'--modern people have a lot of programming that overrides their biology. Yet most people still perform countless selfless acts. Why? What are their motivations?"

"Huh. I guess I don't know."

"It's worth thinking about. But more important to *your* vertical growth is to ask the 'why?' question of yourself. 'Why do *you* do selfless acts?' Or more specifically, 'What was *your* motivation to work at the Habitat house last month?'"

I let it slide that he knew what I'd been thinking and had done last month and contemplated his question. "'Cause my father-in-law asked me to help out, and being unemployed, I had the time?"

Jeff brushed that away. "Surface motivations. What about church three weeks ago?"

I thought back and suddenly realized where my question had come from. "Oh! I hate that. I'd spent three days working on the Habitat house, hanging and floating drywall, my back was killing me, my hands were blistered, and I needed to go back that afternoon because the rain had put them behind schedule. And this guy had the gall to spend almost five minutes during the adult Sunday school class telling us how wonderful he was because he donated two paper bags of last year's fashions clothes to a thrift store. Don't get me wrong, thrift stores are great places, but I was so furious by the time this guy got done I couldn't see straight. He had to make sure to tell us how expensive everything was he donated, piece by piece, and how 'the poor' would value such expensive clothes even if they were a year out of date."

"Calm down, Stanley."

"I can't help it," I replied. "I was angry. I'd spent three backbreaking days working, and he's up there hogging attention for getting rid of stuff he didn't have room in his closet for because he'd gone out and spent his whole paycheck on new clothes! I mean, if you're going to give things away, that's good. But getting up there and crowing about it only for the sake of gathering attention and praise from others... that's not right."

"What is right?"

"Just doing it," I answered. "You just do it because it's right. Not because of all the attention you'll get for doing it."

"There you go. The more a person does a 'selfless act' for the sake of doing the right thing, the more self-realized that person is."

"I must be pretty blasted self-realized, then," I muttered sarcastically.

"Exactly, or else you wouldn't be on this trip with me."

"Lucky me. And if this is the result, maybe I don't want to be self-realized."

Jeff laughed. "The next step is that sometimes you can answer vertical growth questions by intellectualizing like we've done, but at other times, experience is the only answer. Now, let's say somebody pulls over and helps a stranger change their flat tire; afterward, the Good Samaritan drives away feeling great about themselves. What was the Good Samaritan's motivation?"

As if on cue, I saw a car on the side of the road with its trunk lid up and a guy leaning into it. I sighed and looked at Jeff. "What are the chances of that?"

He looked at me, smiling innocently.

"Why am I doing this?" I muttered as I put my blinker on, then changed lanes and slowed the car. "What's my motivation?" I asked as I stopped behind the 1980's land yacht. "Because I have a psycho in the car with me."

"Excellent vertical growth questions, although the answer could use some work."

# Chapter 13

Exasperated, I leaned my head back looking at the car's roof and quietly, but loud enough for him to hear, said, "Why me?"

I got out and slammed the door, purposefully not listening to Jeff laughing as he got out. The traffic rushed by, blowing road debris on me as I walked up the shoulder.

When the guy heard the doors slam, he looked back at us, then straightened, relief clear on his face. He was a very large, muscular young man, somewhere in his early twenties and looked like he needed to get in the sun more. The cheeks of his otherwise pale face were a little red, with a thin coating of sweat giving them a shine from the sun. He must have been here for a while trying to get the tire out. I could understand why no one stopped. With a black bandana holding his long brown hair out of his face, multiple piercings, tattoos all over and a black Marilyn Manson shirt that said, "I'm not a slave to a god that doesn't exist and I'm not a slave to a world that doesn't give a shit.", he didn't give off a warm and fuzzy impression. The reason he was having trouble getting the spare tire out of the trunk was he had only one usable hand, the other was holding up his pants.

He looked at us, gave Jeff's battered face a quick second look but didn't comment on it. "Hey, thanks for stopping. I've never changed a tire and I've gotta meeting in a half-hour."

After reading the shirt, I was wondering how Jeff would handle this.

"You mean no one ever showed you how to do this, friend?"

"No," replied the young man, looking away.

"Really?"

Holding back his irritation--I could see his arm tense, producing an impressive set of muscles--he answered, "I said 'no.'"

Again, with more disbelief, Jeff asked, "Really?"

"Look, I already said 'no'. I gotta get going or I'll be late!"

"Your father never took the time to show you how to change a tire?" Jeff wasn't going to let it drop.

"Can you help me or not? I'll pay you."

"Sure, if you answer my question. Did your father ever try to teach you to change a tire?"

The young man looked down at the road and then out at the passing traffic as he tried to compose himself. I was betting he knew if he got angry, we'd leave, and he needed our help. He looked back at Jeff and flatly said, "He tried. It didn't make any sense, and I had stuff to do. Didn't think I'd ever be on the side of a road like this."

Now that his question was answered, Jeff was once again his cheerful self. "Well, looks like you're on the side of the road, and now, you have a reason to learn. It'll make more sense this time."

"What?" the puzzled man asked.

I could see the rage building in him. His size and appearance intimidated me, but Jeff apparently took no notice.

"Today, my friend, you will learn how to change a tire."

"Hey dude, I gotta get going. I don't have time to learn. Just do it for me and I'll pay ya a hundred bucks."

That was funny. The way Jeff threw around hundred-dollar bills, I knew that offer meant nothing to him.

"Sorry, that's not the way this is going to work. I'll teach you how to change it, or I leave, which means you can figure it out yourself or wait for the next car to stop. But in a world that doesn't care, my friend, you might be here a while." Jeff turned to walk back to my car, and I very willingly followed his lead.

I smiled at Jeff's reference to the kid's Marilyn Manson T-shirt.

"Wait! Okay, but I need to go quick," he called anxiously.

Jeff stopped, gave me a knowing smile as he turned, then walked back to the young man, who towered over him by more than a head. "Well, alright then. What's your name?"

"It's Danger," he replied.

"Quit pretending you're something you're not, friend. Quit *trying* so hard to be someone and just start *being* someone. Your mother and father gave you everything and you threw it in their faces."

Jeff still had the smile while saying this and walked up close to Danger and running his finger across the words of the T-shirt. "They were a slave to you, and they did give a 'care,' and you have the audacity to wear a shirt like that. Now, you're late making a payment to a drug dealer who doesn't care the least little bit about you. It seems you have the world very backwards, friend. When you start caring about the world, you'll find it cares deeply for you."

With intensity and forcefulness, Jeff demanded, "Now, what is your name?"

Danger stood there fidgeting and trying to figure out where to look instead of looking at Jeff, probably wondering how this stranger on the highway knew exactly what had happened with his parents and what he was on his way to do. That had to blow his poor little mind. Finally, with as little defeat as he could fit in his voice, "It's Luke."

"Luke! That's a great name. There was a guy named Luke who wrote a book once. You should read it. Now let's get your tire changed and then we will go take care of your next problem. But first..." Jeff walked back to my car and pulled a T-shirt and belt out of his backpack.

As he walked back to us, all I could do was stare at the things in his hands. Jeff wasn't a small guy, but he wasn't anywhere near Luke's size. Why would he have a shirt that big in his backpack?

Jeff raised his eyebrows at me like he knew what I was thinking and daring me to ask aloud.

I sighed and looked away; I wasn't up to any more weird stuff today.

Jeff tossed the belt and shirt to Luke.

Luke silently changed his shirt and put on the belt.

Once the kid had two useful hands, Jeff stood beside his car and gave instructions that Luke followed.

As Luke was tightening the last lug nut, something behind me caught my attention. I turned to see a Kansas City police car with lights flashing pull up behind my Jetta.

The officer got out, looked back at traffic and walked past my car. "You folks need help or have it under control?"

Jeff straightened as Luke let the jack down. "The tire's changed, but since you're here." He walked to the passenger-side front door of Luke's car, opened the door and reached in.

The officer got stiff and moved his hand closer to his gun.

I did not like where this was going.

Jeff straightened up and looked at him. "Don't worry, it's just drugs, no gun. Can I get it?"

This only confused the officer, but he nodded while keeping his hand on his gun.

Jeff dug under the seat, pulled out a plastic bag and slowly stood up.

I was beyond the point of being surprised at anything Jeff did, but Luke turned paler than he already was. Thankfully, the officer was interested in what was in Jeff's hands, and Jeff's magnetic personality relegated Luke and me to the sideline, where I, at least, was very happy to be.

Jeff walked towards the patrolman who warily waited with his right arm unnaturally tense. Jeff walked past my car and motioned for the officer to follow. Once they were between the Jetta and the patrol car, Jeff started talking. As Jeff talked, the officer kept glancing our way as Luke was trying, unsuccessfully, to appear innocent. Finally, the officer took the bag, got back in his patrol car and drove off.

Jeff walked back, his expression was his usual smile, and addressed Luke. "I think you have an appointment to keep, don't you?" He went back to the passenger door of Luke's car, reached under the seat and pulled out a large wad of money.

Luke's obvious relief the officer was gone was mixed with fury. "No way, dude! I can't go, now! I owe them, and if I don't pay, they'll kill me."

"Trust me." With the look on Jeff's face, Luke had to trust him. That smile and the piercing eyes had an otherworldly authority.

After a few long moments of silence, where Luke's self-preservation warred with Jeff's certainty, Luke finally deflated. "If I die, dude, it's on your head."

"Of course."

I resisted a laugh as Luke turned and got into his car.

When Jeff and I got back to my car, Jeff said, "Follow him."

"If I die, dude," I replied as I climbed into the driver's seat, "not only is it on your head, but Beth will kill you."

Jeff laughed as he dropped the rubber-banded stack of cash onto the center console and buckled his seatbelt.

"And this goes way past Good Samaritan and into outright insanity, friend," I ended mockingly.

"It's all part of the experience, friend," Jeff said, accenting the word 'friend', his eyes full of humor.

"Yeah, right," I grumbled and pulled out into traffic.

We followed Luke's car through a long industrial stretch of highway and onto an exit, then a little way through a suburban neighborhood that had seen much better days. Luke stopped in front of a house that looked pretty much like all the others. The grass was a little longer and the shades pulled, but otherwise, it didn't look like a TV drug house.

I must have been grumbling aloud, because as I pulled up behind Luke, Jeff looked over at me. "Come on, this will be fun."

"Fun? Like the bar was fun? That kind of fun?" I asked, my voice sharp with anxiety.

"At least that much fun. Maybe more. You never know," he said, and I wished he'd quit smiling.

"'You never know?' Is that supposed to make me feel better? If so, it didn't. I think I'll wait here for you." I didn't need another scene like the one from the bar, and from the size of the bundle of cash on the center console, there wasn't any way Jeff could pull this off without somebody dying or getting seriously hurt, and I had a wife and kids to worry about. "I'm happy right here."

He got out, came around, opened my door and pulled me out. "I promise. It'll be fun."

"Yeah, right." But I went with him, mostly because I had to see how he got himself out of this mess.

Even though Luke was trying to put on a brave face, he looked even worse than I felt. When Jeff waved for Luke to take the lead, he said, "Hey, dude. This ain't my idea. I'd have been on my way out of town by now."

Jeff gave an amused shrug, nonchalantly walked to the door, like he didn't have a care in the world, and knocked.

A man with scraggly hair and an oversized mustache opened the door. He was so tall he looked Luke straight in the eye, and then down to the two average citizens, one with a battered face, the other quaking in his shoes.

Jeff said, with his everlasting smile and total calm, "Luke's dad sent me here. He says Luke can't play with you guys anymore."

Luke and I shared a horrified expression, and it briefly crossed my mind to wonder when I'd last updated my will. With that kind of start, there wasn't any way this could turn out well.

The man replied with a couple sentences full of very poor grammar and colorful adjectives.

"That language is part of the reason Luke can't hang out with you kids anymore," Jeff replied. "He's picking up some very bad habits."

The way Jeff was antagonizing the man in front of us, and the two men who had circled around the house and were now standing on the sidewalk behind us, I was wondering who was going to pass out first, me or Luke.

The man with the mustache grabbed Jeff by his shirt-front and threw him inside. Luke and I were herded inside by the guys behind us.

The smell hit me hard. Cigarettes, beer, old food, and things my mildly-wild college days identified. The entry was small for the size of the men surrounding us, and having no other choice, I followed Luke down the short hall and into the kitchen, dim with its shades drawn against the summer sun.

"You're late," a deep voice muttered, "and we don't appreciate unexpected company here."

I turned to see a smaller, thinning-haired, older man sitting at the battered table like it was a throne and looking at Luke like he was an insect, ignoring Jeff and me.

Before Luke could reply, Jeff said, "You aren't presenting a very good argument as to how you're a good influence on Luke." Then he turned to the counter loaded with white powder and a scale. "Hey, are those drugs? Do you have a phone? I need to call the police and let them know."

Jeff was having a great time, Luke and I, not so much.

The balding man at the table stood, gun in hand, and pointed it at Jeff. "Nobody's calling nobody!"

Jeff laughed. "Okay, guys. I was just kidding. Luke's dad didn't send me over here." And then he yelled, "Bang!"

Everyone in the room jumped, but Jeff was laughing uproariously.

"You should've seen your face," he said to the balding man. "Priceless." And laughed some more, ignoring the others in the room.

A voice called out from the angry mutterings behind me, "Shoot the crazy man!" Some part of me had to agree with the sentiment; the world wasn't safe with Jeff on the loose, but I also knew I wasn't getting out of here alive without Jeff, so I hoped he knew what he was doing.

Jeff straightened, took a couple unexpected steps forward and placed his hands on the arm of the balding man, raising the arm until the gun pointed at Jeff's own forehead, then looking serious, smile gone, said, "Yes, shoot me!"

The balding man was obviously as astonished as the rest of us.

"Shoot me!" Jeff commanded into the suddenly silent room.

When the man failed to pull the trigger, Jeff reached up with one hand and pushed the man's trigger finger.

The gun clicked. I jumped, my heart pounding.

Jeff pushed the trigger again.

The gun clicked again.

Jeff took the gun from the stunned man's hand, pointed it at the floor and pulled the trigger. The loud bang made everyone jump and my ears ring. "Huh," he said, looking quizzically at the gun. "It seems to work fine. I wonder what was up with it?"

"It's all part of the experience," I muttered to myself.

He smiled, turned to me and said, "See, Stanley, I told you this would be fun."

"This is the police, open this door!" sounded from the front door, yet, everyone stood there still stunned, and I swallowed some of the curse words Jeff disliked so much. This kept getting better and better.

The door burst open, followed by police in bullet-proof vests and drawn guns. I wasn't surprised in the least when the patrolman from the highway followed them in.

"Well, fun's over," Jeff stated as he tossed the gun on the table, "time to go." Then put his arm up on Luke's shoulder. "Luke, my friend, you just got a 'Get out of jail free' card. Don't waste it. You're riding with us."

Jeff pushed Luke out the door, and I followed, blinking at the bright sunlight, ears ringing and heart still pounding from the gunshot and relieved to still be alive.

The police cleared the way as Jeff smiled and nodded to them. I have no idea what he'd arranged, but we walked out and no one asked us any questions.

Jeff took the keys from my limp hand, got us all into my car with only a minor shuffling of stuff, and drove a few blocks to stop in front of a church that had seen better days. The sign above the doors read, "Church of Undying Love."

It looked like it was a repurposed store on the corner of a block of connected buildings. All the other buildings on the block were boarded up with graffiti covering them. The church portion of the row had mismatched shades of paint covering some of the older graffiti, but new graffiti was sprouting over the attempts to control the spread of the multicolored weed. Some of the windows weren't replaced with plywood but they were the exception.

"I told you those guys didn't need the money, but the guy here does. Come on, I'll introduce you to him." Jeff took the money off the console.

I looked at the wad of money and back at the building. "The guy needs more money than you have there."

Jeff shrugged. "It's a start."

We followed Jeff to the tattered front doors. Bits of plywood were screwed to the doors, I assumed to cover holes. Jeff put his hand on the doorknob and pushed. It was unlocked. The foyer was dim after the bright sunlight. The sanctuary smelled of the altar's flowers and old building, and as we entered, an old, frail but humble looking man rose with effort from his kneeling position at the altar and turned to greet us. White, kinky hair lined his head from ear to ear, leaving the dark, wrinkled skin on his head more pronounced.

"Hello, I'm Reverend Smith. Welcome to my church. How can I help you gentlemen?" He smiled at us excitedly as he spoke.

He was instantly likable. His tone invited us in without conditions.

Jeff reached out and shook his hand. "Hello, Reverend. I'm Jeff, and these are my friends, Stanley and Luke."

I reached out to shake his hand. As I started to grip it I immediately loosened up. His hand was small, and it was clear, didn't have much strength.

Luke held out his hand, and with the strength and size of Luke, I was afraid Luke would unintendedly do damage. But as the white of Luke's hand engulfed the small, dark hand of the Reverend, Luke instinctively relaxed. But what happened next was even more interesting. The Reverend placed his other hand on Luke's, looked up, and locked his eyes on Luke's eyes. He didn't do that with Jeff or me. I was getting used to Jeff naturally drawing people's focus, but Luke was the focal point of this man. There was something happening at a very deep level between Luke and Reverend Smith.

"An interesting story, Reverend Smith." Jeff broke the moment.

The Reverend let go of Luke's hand and turned to Jeff.

Jeff told a much-edited version of the last hour and handed the stack of cash to the wide-eyed minister. Then Jeff turned to Luke. "Your folks gave you a chance at a good life and you threw it away. Today, I'm giving you a new chance. Don't throw this one away. Understand?"

"Yes, sir," Luke answered meekly.

The three of them talked for a few minutes, before Jeff headed out and I followed.

As we were walking out of the sanctuary doors, Jeff turned and said loudly to Luke, "And go see your parents!"

"Yes, sir," Luke replied.

As we walked to the car, I was still riding my adrenalin high, but my curiosity got the better of me and I asked Jeff, "No book for him?"

Jeff looked at me with his smile. "I think he'll find a book in there."

* * *

Back on the highway again, driving through Kansas City evening traffic, I was in my normal state for the last couple of days; my temples throbbed, my mind turned in circles as I thought and rethought the plethora of fragments I was trying to piece together. Luke, the drug house, then the church, Reverend Smith. Self-esteem and selfless acts. None of it seemed connected. Books and money, Sally and Bear, messiah and prophets.

While I agonized, Jeff sat beside me, calmly reading.

As we drove under the sign that marked the Kansas-Missouri border, it occurred to me that, despite my earlier fear that Jeff was a religious fanatic, he hadn't talked about Christianity or other religious ideas with me. He'd only made the messiah-prophet reference that one time, causing me to drive off the road. It was like he was letting me come to terms with all the concepts we'd talked about.

It seemed like a good time to figure out more about who he was. "So, for a messiah, you aren't pushing religion much."

Jeff closed his book and looked at me with his smile. "You going with messiah over prophet?"

"Let's stick with one thing. Seems you'd be pushing your message more."

"I hope I don't *push* anything too much. I hope I teach from the situation at hand and by being an example of love."

Didn't push anything? I tried to think of a time when he did just that. He asked Bear not to swear but turned away afterward. Bear had been the one doing the pushing. I guess you could say he pushed Luke but was also teaching from the situation at hand. As I thought of our conversations, I realized it was always me asking questions; he had never just started pontificating. As much as I wanted to, I couldn't say he had forced anything.

Being an example of love? I meditated on that as I passed a Corolla. In a very strange way, example of love, that is exactly what he was. Sally, Harris, Bear, and now Luke were all better off because of Jeff. As I'd watched Jeff with each person, his love was clear, even when the situations turned stressful. Assuming I was another one of his victims--um, students?--I still wasn't sure about him being an example of love to me. He was nice enough, but 'pain in the butt' seemed a better description than 'example of love.'

"Not buying the messiah thing?" he asked, interrupting my thoughts and putting me on the spot.

I looked at him flustered. "What do you expect? Is that something I should accept after a few parlor tricks? Besides, if that's the case, why choose me to go on this trip? I've never seriously studied the Bible and consider myself agnostic. I'm not even sure there is a God, so the concept of a messiah at all is stretching me." I looked at him wondering how he was taking it, but he remained his usual unflustered self, sitting peacefully beside me, so I returned my attention to the road. "I tolerate going to church because my wife grew up going to that church, and I like the morals it teaches the kids. I think it's good for them to have the foundation."

He looked at me calmly but didn't say anything, so I continued my oration on faith, religion and God. "Some days, I'm sure this whole thing's a cosmic fluke, and other days, I feel there *is* something much greater to all this and there is some meaning to it all. And when I look at Christianity and the other religions, I feel there's a great need for them, but I also feel angry at how they have divided the world."

I paused again and hoped he wouldn't just sit there looking at me again.

He didn't. "Why choose you for this trip? You mean other than the obvious answer of me being a sadist."

"Yes, other than that one. But I don't think you can convince me that isn't your main reason."

"Okay, we'll say that's my main reason." Jeff gently punched my shoulder. "But a close second, you want to know, to believe, but you haven't accepted the definition of God religion has presented you. Which, if you go back to the vertical-growth idea, isn't a bad thing. If all you did was blindly accept what was spoon-fed to you, you'd be as horizontal as the fashion fanatic or that very nice drug dealer we met a few minutes ago."

I shook my head at his attempt at a joke.

"So, let's see if I can help you work some of that out." He paused a moment. "Because you were raised in a Christian church and go to one now, that's whose terminology and examples you understand best. So, I'll work within the scope of Christian teachings, as long as you understand that's only one system, as valid and valuable as many other religions in the world."

"Yeah, I get that. One thing I miss about the church I went to as a kid was their Sunday school class that taught us about all the other religions in the area, and then took us to visit all the different churches. The Buddhist temple was cool."

He nodded. "They are. You should go to the Far East sometime and see real Buddhist temples. They're *very* cool."

"It's on my bucket list if I could get some money saved up."

"Don't despair, Stanley. You never know what the future will bring. But back to religion. The ancient Jews were forbidden to utter their name for God. You've heard the stories about people getting stoned for that?"

"Yeah."

"Stoning people gives the concept a bad rap because not speaking God's name was actually a valuable practice. The Jews felt once you named God, you'd think you'd started to understand God. Typically, once people start to understand something, they start to define it, which is good, except in this one case. God is infinite. Therefore, God can't be defined. Because when one begins to define something, that sets limits on it, but Infinity is limitless. The early Jews didn't want to limit God, so they forbade the speaking of God's name. Most modern churches, however, have no such qualms and spend far too much time defining God and limiting God. You, Stanley, do not accept the limits of God set on Him by religion."

I looked at him questioningly. "So, you're saying my inability to believe, my lack of faith, is good?"

He winked at me. "Don't be so quick to *define* things as good or bad."

I groaned.

He ignored it and continued where he left off. "To add to limiting God, English is a poor language to try to talk about God. Right away, you must assign a gender pronoun to God, requiring Infinity to be either male or female."

"Talk about a big limiting factor."

"Indeed. I think English needs to have a whole new vocabulary before people can use it to talk about God, as God needs to be talked about. According to the Bible, God said 'I am the great I am,' which seems to me to be as much definition as God needs."

"But what does that mean?" I heard myself ask the question and winced with the sudden realization of Jeff's point. "That would be trying to define God, defining Infinity."

"There you go." He turned to face the front and opened his book. "We have hereby finished our discussion of God. Anything else is commentary on how humanity deals with that."

"Thanks," I muttered. I drove more and thought more.

# Chapter 14

Considering how many hours we'd spent in this car over the last couple days, he and I actually hadn't talked that much. But every time we did, I ended up so overwhelmed I had a lot of processing to do.

As I noticed the Walmart-shopping-center sprawl, I realized we were on the 'other side of Kansas City,' so I kept a look-out for a gas station with easy access. I found it a couple exits up, so I got off the highway and pulled up next to a diesel pump.

Jeff handed me a hundred-dollar bill to go pay for it, then got the squeegee and started cleaning the windows.

After going into the thankfully empty store and putting the deposit down on the gas, I walked back to the car and Jeff had already started pumping the diesel.

"Did you buy a lottery ticket, friend?" he asked with his smile.

"Very funny."

"Did you leave the money in there for the next people?"

"No. You didn't say to," I said leaning my hip against the rear hatch, "and I wasn't going to do that with your money."

He shrugged and replied, "Bummer, now we have to stand in line again."

"Why don't you get a credit card and pay at the pump? You know, they've the technology to do that now."

He gasped. "Credit cards? Do you know how many lives those things are destroying? It's best to stay away from them."

Thinking about how much debt I had on mine, I wished I'd been able to stay away from them, but I had to feed the kids, and my credit cards were the only thing allowing me to do that. I was glad Jeff was paying for gas this trip; otherwise, it'd be going on my card, too. With the horrendous interest rates I was paying, I knew of one life credit cards were ruining. The worst part was, it was my fault. To blame the credit card companies would be like blaming fast food for your kid being fat.

That got me thinking. This gas station had a fast food restaurant attached to it. We could eat there.

But that thought was distracted by a car with four young men in it pulling into the station. It was one of those vehicles with an unnatural balance of form and function. The owners had spent tons of money trying to add form to the car, but in the process, removed much of its function. This vehicle had massive chrome wheels with unimaginably low-profile tires which had almost no clearance in the wheel wells.

I watched them drive over a speed bump on the way to the pump. They stopped before the bump and eased over it.

The 1940's Lincoln Continentals used to carry their spare tire on the back of the trunk in an attractive wheel-shaped compartment. In later years, the compartment was used for decoration and called a continental kit. The car that had finally inched over the speed bump had two fake continental kits, one on top of the trunk and one vertically behind the trunk. On the hood was a massive gaudy, ill-fitting hood ornament. Other than that, the car was rusted out, in dire need of a paint-job and basically a total piece of junk. The rims probably cost more than the car did.

Shaking my head as I watched the vehicular comedy come towards the pump next to us, I mumbled to myself, "Goofy mobile." I'd always called them that because they made absolutely no rational sense.

Jeff looked at me and grinned. "A very fitting term."

I looked over at him returning the grin, surprised I had said it that loud.

In character with all goofy mobiles, this vehicle had its windows down and the passengers of the car made the assumption everyone around shared their musical taste.

The driver got out attempting to look cool as he tried to work the pump handle, gas cap and paying at the pump all with only one hand because the other was holding up his pants. Form over function, exactly like his vehicle. He thought he looked cool, his friends might have thought he looked cool, everyone else laughed silently or felt sorry for him.

Jeff didn't seem to share their taste in profanity-laced music and leaned around the pump to address the young man. "Hey, friend, do you think you can turn your radio down? It seems you and I prefer different music."

The driver looked at Jeff, defiance easy to read in his expression. "What?"

Jeff politely repeated his request, "Would you please turn down your radio? Not everyone shares your taste in music."

The man's defiance grew and he loudly proclaimed, "Man, you've offended me! I don't know you from nobody, and you're telling me to turn off my music."

I was simply blown away at the man's reaction, at his self-centered attitude, which was being fed by his cohorts in the car laughing and egging him on.

With his typical smile, Jeff calmly questioned the man, "I have offended you? Really?"

"Yah, you offended me."

Jeff nodded with a questioning look. "How interesting. You force everyone here to listen to your profanity-laced music, where the main subject is about abusing women, and I have offended you? You almost have me speechless, friend."

Now the guy was getting angry. "Shut your mouth, before I bust up your face worse than the last guy did."

Jeff, of course, took no notice of the threat. "So, let me get this straight. If I played music you didn't want to hear, and you asked me to turn it down, I should be offended."

The guy walked towards Jeff pointing his finger at Jeff's chest. "If you played what I don't want to hear, I'd break your fingers and then make you change it."

I wasn't sure what was going to happen, but I knew it'd be interesting.

In response to the physical aggression, Jeff merely nodded with a knowing smile. "I see. Let's see how your plan works."

Jeff slowly raised his hand above his shoulder, the man readied to defend himself, I almost hoped Jeff was going to deck him, and then Jeff snapped his fingers.

His would-be assailant was confused at first, but then quickly turned to look at his goofy mobile in horror. I smiled because Jeff had done something better than decking the guy. I had no clue how, but he'd changed the music. It was still a rap song, but it was one I knew. Cooper and I had watched it repeatedly on YouTube. The chorus came blasting out of the speakers, "Please, pull your pants up!" by the rapper Six8.

The driver yelled at his three passengers for changing the music. The man in the front passenger seat yelled he didn't do that and was frantically trying to stop or switch the song.

Jeff yelled over the music, "Thanks for changing it. I actually like that song."

All the people at the gas station, who'd been trying to ignore these obnoxious fools, now turned and smiled at us.

"It looks like other people like it too. Look at all the attention you're getting."

The passenger was still frantically trying to shut the radio off, but it wouldn't shut off.

The driver hung up the pump handle, opened the driver's door and slid in. He tried to start the car, but it just cranked without firing.

Jeff hung up our pump handle, closed the gas tank door, and then leaned down to look in the window of the form-over-function car and said, "Have a nice evening, gentlemen. I've decided I like your musical taste."

They only looked at him with anger and embarrassment.

He grinned and then turned to me. "I'll go deal with the cashier, while you move the car over in front of the restaurant?"

"Okay." As I did, I was thinking about how much better Jeff's strategy worked than decking the guy.

Pulling out my phone, as I waited for Jeff, I decided to give Beth a call. I wanted to talk to her with some privacy. As it rang, I was thinking about how to explain today.

Beth answered, "Hi, Stanley. Glad you were able to call this evening," with a tone of sarcasm.

"Me, too. We're going to be driving for a while tonight, so I wanted to call when Jeff wasn't around. We've stopped for gas and dinner."

She interrupted, "Before we get talking, Thing 1 wants to talk to you."

I heard her say "Here," and then Cooper was on the phone.

*"I'm so glad my Dad is calling.*
*He's gone away and the sky is falling.*
*Thing 2 has spent the whole day bawling.*
*You'd better come back soon, without stalling."*

I nodded in fatherly approval. "Very nice, Cooper. You spend the day working on it?"

"Not *all* day," he replied, offended.

"Guess I should have been working on one, too."

He hurriedly said, "Maybe next time. Gotta go. Here's Mom."

Knowing he already had the phone away from his ear, I quickly and loudly said, "I love you!" and heard a distant, "I love you."

Beth was back on. "He's been waiting for you to call all day for that. Now he has a YouTube video that's more important."

"So, everything's normal, is what you are telling me?"

"Pretty much. How about your trip? Is everything normal?" She tried to joke, but I could hear the hesitation in her voice.

"Hmmm, where do I start?"

Jeff exited from the convenience store part of the station, saw I was on the phone, waved at me. I waved back, and he went into the restaurant part.

Beth's voice in my ear stated the obvious, "Start at the beginning."

I thought back to the hotel after our last call this morning. "Well, not only can he predict the future, he can open locked doors. You remember me talking about the book he gave me?"

"Something about a square and a sphere?"

"That's the one. This may sound crazy, but I think he's trying to tell me that if I compare him and me, it's like the sphere in comparison to the square. So, is he basically a fourth-dimensional being? That would explain how he can tell the future and open locked doors."

Exasperated, she said, "Stanley! You've been watching too many sci-fi movies."

"I know that's what it sounds like, but it makes sense. Pain doesn't even seem to bother him. He wasn't even bothered by me slugging him after he kissed me." Then immediately wished I'd have thought before I'd said that.

"What?" she exclaimed.

I tried to backtrack and fix the previous sentence. "No. Not like that! Nothing like that! I had a headache, and he kissed me on the forehead. I had the most bizarre feeling in my head, like fingers were moving around tinker toys, and then the headache was gone. In fact, I felt great afterward. I wasn't tired or anything."

"He can heal, too?"

"Well, headaches at least." And then I thought about his statement about the mud. "And he said he can cure blindness. He said something about making mud from spit to cure blindness isn't going over so well."

Now she wasn't happy. "Does he think he's Jesus or something?"

"Well, not Jesus exactly." As I still didn't know what to think of any of that, I changed the subject. "We had an interesting discussion on people's ability to handle wealth, we talked about vertical versus horizontal growth, and we helped a guy change his flat tire."

"Out doing good deeds with Jesus?"

"Well, more than that." I figured I would go for broke. "The guy with the flat tire was a drug dealer who owed money to these people. We went to a drug house and Jeff had it raided by the police while we were there. Then Jeff had this guy point a gun at his head and he pulled the trigger but the gun didn't fire. And then Jeff took the gun and shot it into the floor and it worked fine." I thought a second. "He has absolutely no fear. He walked right up to that house, excited about what was going to happen."

"Oh, Stanley."

"And then he took the guy who had the flat tire, Luke, like from the Bible, to a church down the road. And like the guy at the bar, the flat-tire guy and the one we dropped off at the church were two different people."

The anxiety level in her voice was high. "This has gone too far, Stanley. You need to get away from him."

I understood her concern, but that wasn't the right answer. "I hear you, Beth, and the thought has crossed my mind more than once. But for some strange reason, this feels right. Like I'm supposed to be with him."

Beth didn't respond right away, then finally said softly, "I'm not there, so I'll have to trust you know what's right."

"It is, Beth. I truly believe it is."

She didn't respond right away again. "Okay. I don't know what else to say about it." She paused again. "Here, Alice wants to talk to you."

I talked to my sweet six-year-old, Alice, for a little bit before saying good-bye to everybody and hanging up. It was going to be a long two months without my family. I then headed into the restaurant and located Jeff.

As I sat down, he asked, "Everything okay?"

"I guess. She's pretty worried about me." I then looked at him. "About me being with you."

"She loves you. That's good."

I started eating the meal he'd ordered for me and looked out the window at the guys who were still trying to get their car started and the radio off. "So, what book are you going to give those guys?"

He looked out the window at the men, then with a half-smile he said, "Do you think I can find a copy of *Green Eggs and Ham* nearby?"

Laughing, I answered, "I have a couple copies at home. I should've brought one."

Then he turned more serious. "It's sad to see. There's a large culture of mega-followers out there. I told you before, when Jesus walked the Earth the people were spiritually advancing, but technically very primitive."

"Yeah, I remember."

"Now, humanity is technology advancing, but most of this world's population is benefiting from the greatness of a small number of people. And most of the population consumes the advancements of others with no appreciation, no gratitude, and most sadly, with no sense of wonder."

I nodded. "I'm old enough to remember the days before cell phones, and my kids take them completely for granted."

"Even worse is how much of this amazing technology that's used for such trivial applications. It's put into products consumers will buy but offer no value to them. It's like taking a Rolls Royce and plowing a field. The tool is magnificent, and the task it's being used for is trivial. The only difference in my example is, plowing a field is worthwhile. Using microcircuits and transistors to create an electronic keychain pet is pointless, yet people still buy them."

"Sorry," I said, thinking of all the pointless, cheap gadgets Beth and I had bought the kids that ended up in the trash after a short time.

"It's something to be aware of." He ate more, looking out the window. "Our friends out there at the pump are prime examples of users of technology who themselves give nothing back. They reject knowledge and education, and live immersed in the shallowness of image."

A couple of thoughts hit me right away and I looked at Jeff. "Horizontal growth?"

He nodded and said, "Very little growth of any kind. Mostly stagnation."

I added my second thought. "Back to our brain discussion. What were the traits you said were in the primitive part of the brain?"

Jeff rattled them off. "Status, power, control, territory, sex, personal gain, and survival."

I looked back out the window at the car and the picture was clear, and not just for them. I asked, "But that applies to so many people, and I'm not leaving myself off that list."

He looked me straight in the eye. "Why do you take guitar lessons?"

This guy freaks me out sometimes; I'd never told him that. I tried to switch my thoughts from how he could even ask the question, to his actual question. After a brief pause, I answered, "I don't know. I guess because I'm so bad at it." Then his point was clear. "I think that part of my brain needs the work-out. Vertical growth?"

He looked at me with an expression that had so much depth. It read of acceptance, love, and understanding in a way no one had ever looked at me. "I rest my case. We all function at some level in our primitive brain, but it's the push to expand our minds, to exercise our modern brain, that'll drive humanity to the next level."

I turned around and looked at the people in the restaurant, normal people going about their normal day-to-day lives. I knew I spent most of my time and thought process getting through each day. Other than attempting to play the guitar, I couldn't think of anything I did to use my modern brain.

Jeff looked out the window, again, and as a statement of fact rather than opinion, he said, "The driver dropped out of high school as a freshman, reading at a third-grade level. His math was worse. He has a whole culture around him that supports him and respects him, as long as he projects the right image."

"What can you do for him?" I asked.

He looked over at me, picked up his cup, and took a drink from the straw. "If you stand on a chair and someone else is standing on the floor, it's much easier for him to pull you down than it is for you to pull him up. Those four men out there have a lot of people pulling them off the chair, and no one strong enough to pull them back up. I have plans, just not today at a gas station."

My phone rang. I pulled it out, and it wasn't in my contact list, so I handed it to Jeff, and then took the last bite of my hamburger.

We were done eating, so we got up and headed out while he started the conversation.

Jeff answered, "Oh, my face is fine; it doesn't hurt much at all." He looked at me and smiled.

I realized it was Bear, the biker.

"You don't need to apologize any more. It was a very small price to pay to give you your life back and to give you your father back." Pause. "You know, I have actually never read that book."

I turned and looked at him in shock.

"I have read other Louis L'Amour books but not that one."

We got in my car. I started the car and backed out as he

continued.

"I like how black and white his books are. The good guys are strong, tough men with unbending character and the bad guys are strong tough men with no scruples at all." Pause. "Once I saw that book, I figured it would mean something to you." Pause. "That's the right thing to do, and I will support you every step of the way." Pause. "Hold on a second. Stanley, stop a moment."

Unable to resist the second act of the play, I stopped abreast of the goofy mobile and Jeff rolled down his window and leaned out.

Their radio was now playing Maddline's song "Tighty-Whities," another one of Cooper's and my favorite videos. The man in the driver's seat was trying to start the car and the other three guys were out, looking very uncomfortable and trying to figure out how to get the car started and the radio turned off.

Jeff called out over the deafening radio, "I gotta go, gentlemen, and I hope our next meeting is more pleasant." And abruptly the music stopped.

In the stunned silence, the man in the driver's seat turned the key, and the car started. He looked at the original driver with a perplexed expression, and then demoted himself over to his assigned seat on the passenger side.

The driver, the one who'd threatened Jeff, looked at Jeff with a mixture of anger and confusion but said nothing as he got into the car.

Jeff waved at them as the other two guys hurriedly got into the car, then pulled his head back in and rolled up the window. "Onward, Stanley." And he put the phone back up to his ear. "Okay, I can hear you now." Pause. "Yeah, it was loud. Now, don't forget you have another phone call to make. That's all I ask of you." Pause. "I love you too, friend. It's going to work out much better than you think. You can trust me on that. Bye." Jeff hung up and put the phone in the cupholder.

I waited a minute as I pulled back onto the highway. "Well?"

Jeff was staring off into space, with a look of satisfaction on his face. "He's going to be fine." He nodded. "Yes. He's going to be just fine."

I knew I wouldn't get anything out of Jeff, so I kept my thoughts to myself.

Jeff had changed so many people's lives on this trip, and I couldn't help but believe the young men at the gas station would end up profoundly changed, even if I couldn't see the mechanism behind their change. But *I* was still the same. At least I still felt the same. I was still 'me.'

Did Bear still feel like himself, even though he clearly wasn't? I mean, the guy could now easily say "I love you" and mean it, which I suspect had never happened before he met Jeff.

If Jeff changed me that much, would I still be *me*?

I wasn't sure I wanted to find out. In fact, I was pretty sure I didn't. I simply wanted to get to Bethlehem, do a good job at work, pay my bills, and get home to my family.

A weird little voice in the back of my head chirped up, "Horizontal growth."

Yeah, I told it, I'm all for horizontal growth.

"Liar," the little voice replied.

I turned on the CD player to drown it out.

# Chapter 15

We drove for a while listening to the music. I was glad I was heading east because the setting sun was glaring in my rearview mirror and a minor adjustment fixed the problem.

The obnoxious voice had finally shut up, and my thoughts turned to various things Jeff had said.

The conversation I'd had with Beth, where I avoided the question of Jeff thinking he was Jesus, made me want to dig deeper into that. I was sitting here with a guy who said he was either a prophet or a messiah--he would let me pick which one--and what I'd seen him do added support to it. So, if he genuinely was, now was the time to get answers. Answers to tough questions.

A few Sundays before the old minister died, he preached a sermon that rubbed the thorn in my side about Christianity. He'd brought up one of the questions about Christianity no one had ever been able to answer for me, one that hampered my ability to believe like the others in church did.

I turned off the music and said, "A little while back the minister gave this big long sermon about Jesus being the ultimate blood sacrifice. I just don't get it. Why would a God of love require a blood sacrifice in the first place? Others seem to believe it so easily, but it doesn't make sense to me. Why did Jesus have to die?"

Jeff closed his book and looked over, unfazed by my sudden and pointed question. "That's a big one for you, isn't it?"

"Yes, one of the main ones. I mean, God created all the rules. So why would a God, supposedly a God of love, demand an act that's so brutal and puts him at the same level as the gods of other religions of the time?"

He nodded. "It is a big one for others, too. And one of the main ones I am here to explain. The strange thing is, as big as the concept seems, the basics of it aren't that hard to understand." He waited briefly to give me time to prepare. "It's obvious Jesus came to make changes. Right?"

"Sure."

"Moses came to make changes. Right?"

I shrugged. "Okay, sure."

"Change can only happen in stages. Drastic changes can't happen overnight and expect humanity to be able to handle them. So, the process is: change a little, wait for that change to have its effect and the waves of it to smooth out, change some more and wait for the waves to smooth out. The changes brought by the Mosaic Law worked for the people of Moses' time. Jesus came when Moses' waves had smoothed out and made more waves."

Jeff paused, apparently waiting for me.

I wasn't sure if he was waiting for me to ask a question, or to think about what he had said. I didn't have any questions and so far, what he said wasn't revolutionary to me. "Okay."

"God doesn't require blood sacrifices. But as you stated, most religions of the time *did* require them and so did the people, because that's what they understood."

"Huh. Hadn't thought of it that way."

"Change can only move so far, so fast, and it has to be appropriate to the people being changed. The only way to move them into their next stage of understanding was for Jesus to be the ultimate blood sacrifice for them, the last blood sacrifice. God didn't require it; the people of the time required it."

I put up my hand. "Hold on, hold on. Let me think for a minute." What he was saying *was* revolutionary to me. God worked at the level of the people of the time. Jesus was an instrument of change to allow society to let go of practices and beliefs which were holding them back from having a more mature understanding and relationship with God. "Wow. That makes sense." I looked over at Jeff, surprised; I didn't think anybody would ever be able to explain it to me.

He wasn't done. "Plus, if Jesus would've only told stories--very good stories, by the way—and performed a few miracles, his impact would've been minimal. He'd have been noted as merely another prophet if noted at all. But, because of his crucifixion, he made the major headline news of the time, and the stories he told became more than stories. Therefore, Jesus' teachings were noticed and he made big waves. Now, his waves are settling and it's time for more waves. It's time for more change."

I was stunned. I'd asked one of the main questions that had thwarted Christianity for me, the question no one had been able to answer with any real meaning, and Jeff had explained it to me in less than two minutes, in a way that didn't even boggle my mind. It made sense. "It can't be that simple. You're telling me the practice of blood sacrifice was holding people and religion back, and Jesus died to end that?"

He grinned at me. "For that question, yes, it's that simple. But don't assume Jesus was here to do only that. His greatness is so much more."

"Yeah, I get that. But thanks for answering my question. That's pretty cool to understand it."

"No problem."

As we passed the sign informing us we were entering Boone County and about to cross the Missouri River, I thought about all of this, then I turned to Jeff. "So, are you going to have to die to make your message heard?"

I'm not sure why I asked that. I was still extremely torn as to what to make of Jeff, or of Jesus for that matter. He sure seemed okay with Jesus and his own role, but I knew I had a long way to go. So maybe I was asking to see how he saw things progressing.

He smiled calmly. "Times are different now because of Jesus. I don't need to be a blood sacrifice because he did that for me, just as he did it for you."

Now I got to smile at him. "I'm glad to hear that. One massive question resolved in my head. That's enough for tonight. I'll let you read your book." I looked at the Missouri River as we crossed over.

"Stanley," said Jeff and I glanced at him. He had a more serious look on his face than I was used to. "Don't sweat the question of who I am. Even Jesus' disciples questioned him, didn't understand him. I hereby relieve you of that burden."

Confused I looked at him. "But that leaves me with the choice of you being crazy or a liar. I don't believe you are either one of those, so I have to find a way to believe you are the third choice."

His expression gently gave the message I was wrong. "No, you don't 'have' to believe anything until you believe it. Spending your life trying to believe something you don't believe would make you a liar and possibly drive you crazy. Believe when you believe and not before."

I had to laugh at that. "I'm beginning to believe that believing in you is believable."

His expression returned to his usual smile. "Believe me, I believe you're going to be fine, friend."

I drove on, wondering if Jesus had been this cool to hang out with.

It was after eleven at night, and I was exhausted when we finally made it to our planned stop on the outskirts of St. Louis. I was glad to pull into a hotel parking lot and closed my eyes as Jeff went in to get the rooms.

Once in my room, I threw my duffel bag to the floor and collapsed onto the bed. As I lay there, I couldn't help but feel a little depressed. Tomorrow was the last day of the trip. This very strange stranger I'd reluctantly picked up three days ago, with the plan to get rid of him as soon as I could, was now someone I didn't want to exit from my life. He'd obviously chosen me for this trip, but I still had no idea why.

The rest of the trip to Bethlehem, PA would take about fifteen hours. Our plan was to drive all day and make it there late tomorrow, Saturday, night. Which was good because I'd have Sunday to rest before starting work. But it also meant I had only fifteen hours left with the man who'd had such a profound effect on me in such a short time, and I had so many questions.

Most of my questions were unformed though. I needed to get them organized in my head.

With a sigh, I heaved myself off the bed. As I got ready, I tried to form questions to ask Jeff tomorrow, but no specific ones came to me.

I went to sleep with a busy mind and was surprised I fell asleep right away.

\* \* \*

I got up in the morning still thinking, still trying to form good questions. I put all of that on hold when I got a text from Beth saying she was up if I wanted to call. I wouldn't really have another time to talk to her in private so, since she was up, this was a great time to talk.

It was hard to tell if it was humor or worry in her voice, as she started inquiring about the trip. "Well, I'm almost afraid to ask, but how's the trip going?"

"Do you remember Dan's sermon a few weeks before he died about Jesus being the ultimate blood sacrifice and I was complaining to you that it didn't make any sense?"

Beth responded, "Okay, sure. I remember something about that. It isn't that uncommon of a topic. Why do you ask?"

"Jeff answered it as clear as can be in a couple of minutes," and I went on to explain what Jeff had said about people needing the sacrifice, not God.

Beth was silent on the other end. "That even answers it for me, and I didn't even know I had a question with it. That makes so much sense and it fits with the Scriptures. Who is this guy? I mean what's his training? What's his background?"

Once again, Beth demonstrated her superior wisdom. Why hadn't I asked Jeff those questions? "I really don't know." I knew a bunch of little things about him, but none of it would give him any credibility in Beth's eyes. I'd been with the guy for three days now and hadn't asked any obvious questions. I tried to redeem myself, "I'll make sure I have those answers tomorrow."

"Stanley, Stanley, Stanley. You never cease to amaze me."

All husbands know that isn't a compliment.

"Do you even know what he's doing? What he's planning? Why you're on this trip with him?"

I thought for a minute. "He did say that the explanation of blood sacrifices is part of the message he is here to deliver."

"So, he's a messenger from God then? My husband, the guy who sleeps through sermons, is on a road trip with a messenger from God. Interesting. Can't wait to tell all of my friends about this." Sarcasm is one of her gifts and usually makes me laugh.

"Guess I'll try to narrow it down today. I'll have to decide between alien, multi-dimensional being, messiah, prophet, or messenger from God."

"I can't believe you didn't throw 'mutant' in there."

Cooper and I watch all of the mutant superhero movies and cartoons we can find. "Great point! I can't believe I forgot that one either."

I could visualize her shaking her head on the other end of the phone. It was going to be a long two months without my family. As much as Beth and I harassed each other we had a very fun relationship.

We ended the call and as I got ready to go I tried hard to think about what I would ask Jeff today, beyond the answers Beth wanted.

Not obvious ones such as why there was evil in the world. That one had never bothered me. There can be no good without evil. Evil was what made you know what good was. It's like the time I had severe knee pain and couldn't walk. I'd never appreciated how wonderful walking was until I couldn't walk.

Anyway, that question was okay in my mind.

Before I could come to any conclusions, Jeff knocked on the door. We headed off to get some breakfast. It was quiet because I was still trying to form a good question, and Jeff didn't push the conversation. Our whole trip he hadn't. For a guy who had a message for the world, he sure didn't work hard to get it out. Breakfast was uneventful, Jeff left his usual tip, and I was wondering what the adventure would be today. I didn't have much time with him, I couldn't waste it.

Soon after we were on the road, Jeff asked, "Can we drive past the Arch? I always like seeing it."

I liked seeing it too. Someday, I'd like to go inside it. "Sure, it isn't too far out of the way."

As we passed by the Arch, Jeff watched it with his typical glow for life. "It's amazing what can be done with an opposable thumb and the ability to reason."

I watched the Arch recede in my mirror, as we continued over the Mississippi River, heading out of St. Louis. "This isn't what I expected when I picked you up in California."

"Do you still wish you had gotten the window up at the traffic light before I walked up?"

Dang, he knew what I was thinking then, so he must know what I am thinking now. Why doesn't he simply answer the questions I have and save me all the anxiety?

"Because you need to ask the questions. Me answering them isn't as important as you asking them. By the time you have organized your thoughts enough to form a clear question in your head, you've thought about it long enough that the answer will mean something."

"I guess that makes sense. But why did you answer that question before I asked it?"

"You weren't going to ask that one, but I thought it was a good one to answer. So, go ahead, ask the big one. Even if you don't ask it exactly right, I'll still give you the answer you're really looking for." He seemed to enjoy playing mind games with me.

"Okay, okay, I think I have it how I want it asked anyway. This is another one that has kept Christianity at a distance for me. No one has ever given me a good answer. I get a lot of 'it's a matter of faith' or 'who are you to question the ways of God?' or a bunch of other cop-out answers."

"Okay. I can tell you already this one will be different from yesterday. It will take longer to explain. But lay it on me," he instructed.

"How can a God of love use such a primitive control system as reward and punishment for our actions and beliefs on Earth to determine our eternity in the afterlife?" I think that got my issue out.

"In other words, 'why heaven and hell?'"

"Yeah."

He nodded. "In some ways, we've already covered that, but there is a part of it that'll be a shocker to you. As I've said before, and this, in itself, is an extremely important message. Jesus talked to the people of his time in a way they could understand, at a level they could understand, and only the amount they could understand.

"He couldn't tell them everything, any more than you could be expected to walk into a nuclear physics class one day and then build a nuclear power plant the next day. Jesus came to lay another few rounds of blocks in the building of God's church and did it in a way that when he wasn't around people could still understand it."

I interrupted, "So you're telling me, what has happened after Jesus died is what he intended? The Crusades? The dark ages? Salem witch trials? World War I and II?"

"No, it doesn't mean they did exactly what God wanted, but as I said before, the things that go wrong help you understand how to make things right. Some things were messed up and some things went pretty darn good. And they are all part of the key, so now humankind is ready to build on what was done right and learn from what was done wrong."

"Like the good and evil thing? Bad needs to happen so we can learn from it, and it also gives us another reason to appreciate the good in our lives."

"Exactly. Some places in the world haven't really changed that much from when Jesus walked around. Religion plays the highest role in their lives and everything can and must be explained through religion. If someone tries to explain to these people, eating food with high levels of saturated fat is bad for them and explain why, they'll still eat it and eat a lot of it. Now, if they're told God will punish them for eating unclean things and then give them a list of supposedly unclean food, they won't eat the food. With these people, religion plays a bigger role in life than logic and reason."

"So, for us, it's the opposite?" I asked.

"Hardly. Now the two need to join. Religion and science--two parts of the same thing--have the same end goal, to answer the how and why of our existence. God put humans here and God made them curious. God made them ask questions and seek answers.

"The story of Adam and Eve is the prime example of that. Humanity is here to seek knowledge and grow but there are consequences to that. Where humanity is struggling right now is because it's trying to keep religion and science separate, which is like trying to keep water from mixing with water. It's an impossible task and will drive them nuts. To look from a religious point of view and say science is wrong, or to look from a scientific point of view and say religion is wrong, is nuts, pure insanity. When they let the water mix with the water, they--everyone--will start to comprehend God the way God truly is."

I butted in, "That conflict has always seemed strange to me."

"That is one of the reasons you're sitting here."

I was wondering what the other ones were, but before I could ask, he continued.

"You should read Francis Collin's book *The Language of God.* He was in charge of the Human Genome Project and is an evangelical Christian. It's an interesting book which does a good job of trying to dissolve the conflict between science and religion. But anyway, you ready to go on with answering your question?"

I replied with a nod.

"The best way to describe our existence in this realm is filtered. We can't see God in all God's glory and we can't even begin to understand God's wholeness. The churches say God is infinite but infinity is far too much for anyone to comprehend."

"That seems like a strange statement. Infinity is everything and forever," I said puzzled.

He smiled, "Like I said, humans cannot comprehend what that means. You can say the words but they're just words and a shadow of meaning. The realm you and other humans occupy is filtered from the next realm. We can get a glimpse of the next realm, but it's nothing like this. Its intensity dwarfs your experience here. Everything is amplified from the point of view of someone crossing over." He looked at me. "Dying." He paused to let me think.

He kept saying "next realm" and that was confusing me. "You mean Heaven or Hell when you say next realm?"

"That is how Jesus described it to a simpler people."

I interrupted, "But now we're ready to subtract bigger numbers from smaller numbers, right?"

He didn't mind the interruption. "Yep, but that doesn't mean it is going to be easy. What do you visualize when you think of Heaven or Hell?"

"I think most peoples' vision of Hell was mostly invented by Dante in his book *Divine Comedy* in the *Inferno* section. I know that's what comes to my mind. For Heaven, you know, streets of gold, mansions, I guess kind of a Roman type of architecture. I have no illusions those images are close to what they're actually like. They're merely the images that are portrayed by art, media, and pictures from Sunday school."

"You're right, they aren't even close. And what it actually is can't be comprehended by beings occupying this realm or dimension."

Whoa! "Like *Flatland*? Where the sphere is trying to explain things to the square?"

He smiled knowingly at me but waited for me to keep going, so I grasped at the next logical thing he was driving at. "Are you saying the next realm, Heaven and Hell, when we die, we go to the fourth dimension?"

With a big smile, he nodded his head up and down and said, "No, but that's an awesome analogy. It's awesome enough that I'd almost say 'yes,' but it's still too simplistic. But for the next stage in human understanding of the divine plan it works great, so let's use it."

That didn't help me too much or leave me feeling like I was onto the truth. "Come on, Jeff. Don't play games with me."

"Sorry, can't help it. The truth is still way too much for you or anyone else at this stage."

Again, I interrupted, "Other than you?"

"Like Jesus, I'm not at 'this stage.' Even though I see an exponentially clearer version of God's truth, the wholeness of it is so infinite I can only see a small portion of it."

He waited for me to interrupt again but I just looked out the front window and watched the broken center line stripe whiz by as I thought about him comparing himself to Jesus again and placing himself as a being advanced enough to truly understand God.

He continued, "Go back to *Flatland* and imagine what the square saw when he went with the sphere to the sphere's third-dimension."

I still didn't respond but did think about that. It would probably be next-to-impossible for the two-dimensional square to comprehend the concept of *height*. It reminded me of the research done on animals, in which they raised some animals in an environment with only horizontal lines and when the animals grew up they literally couldn't see vertical lines. If I could even see the next spatial dimension, I couldn't imagine what it might look like to me, let alone if I could make any sense of it at all.

Jeff gave me a lot of time before he asked, "Can you imagine Jesus having this conversation with people of his time?"

I switched my mind to imagine Jesus explaining these concepts to illiterate people with no formal education, in a society that was still over a thousand years before algebra. "No, I guess I can't see that happening."

"Exactly. So back to what I was saying about the next realm. The realm we're in is highly filtered from the next. When you go to the next realm, usually by way of death, you'll take what you are here with you."

"No suitcases of gold?"

He laughed. "No, no gold. Instead, you take what is in your heart with you. You take your *soul* with you. If you're a person of love, you take love with you, and it's unfiltered. If you're a person of hate and anger, you take that with you, unfiltered or from the perspective here, it is amplified."

I watched the cornfields zoom by and pondered. Jeff was right, this question was not as easy to answer as the previous one and it was a shocker. "So, when we die and our soul or heart, or whatever you want to call it, is filled with anger we go to the next dimension where that anger is amplified?"

"I prefer 'realm' over 'dimension.' Dimension brings a bunch of sci-fi concepts with it, but you can use that one if you want. But yes, that's right."

I continued, "That would be terrible. In fact..."

Jeff nodded and smiled knowing what I was going to say.

"...that would be Hell."

"And if you're consumed with love here?" he asked.

"Amplified love? That would be beautiful." I looked over at him wide-eyed. "It would be Heaven in the same place."

He gave me a look of satisfaction. "You got it, friend! It's not a reward or punishment based on judgment; it's a reality. And you can't fool that reality. To put it another way, you step on the scale in the morning and don't like what you see, so you go to your closet and put on something with vertical stripes which may make you look thinner. When you step on the scale, it doesn't care if the stripes make you look thinner, it doesn't judge you, the number you look at will be the same."

I was getting his flow. For many of the Christians I know, it's more important to be perceived as a Christian than to live Jesus' message of love. Televangelists had driven that point home repeatedly as they kept getting caught doing exactly what they preached against. I added to his analogy, "If you change the weight number on your driver's license and then go weigh yourself, the scale still tells you the same thing."

"Right. You can tell the world how much weight you've lost, and then weigh yourself, the scale will have taken no notice, you still weigh the same. You haven't been judged by gravity and you can't fool gravity. Going to the next realm is the same. You make it Heaven or Hell by the contents of your own heart, without judgment. It may seem like you are rewarded or punished, but you do it to yourself. Calling yourself a Christian or doing the occasional good deeds for people changes nothing if, in your soul, you're a person of anger, hate, and resentment. Only when you truly know love, only when you truly understand what Jesus was telling the world what love is, will you enter Heaven. What Jesus taught about love and how to live your life was timeless. Jesus' message of love is the gate to Heaven."

Jeff had done it again. He'd taken one of my main problems I had with what Christianity taught and made it clear to me. But now I had a lifetime of spiritual healing ahead of me; I needed to work this into my thought patterns to try to replace the lifetime of being told something which didn't make sense to me, yet afraid not to believe for fear of eternal damnation. Beth's church used fear as a way to get me to believe, but love was all I needed. What Jeff said made so much sense, yet I knew I wasn't going to change overnight; I had a lot of healing to do from the damage of well-intended, but wrong, people.

"You good?" he asked.

I looked over at him in a new light. Was he really who he proclaimed himself to be? Messiah started rising over multi-dimensional being. Well, actually, the two started becoming one. "No, I mean yes. I'm good," I said as I looked at him with a confused expression. "I need to think now."

He winked at me and started reading again.

# Chapter 16

I drove and thought for a long time. The sun was giving way to overcast, which was nice because it was easier on my eyes. I drove until I heard the sound every driver hates to hear, the 'thump, thump' of a tire that just went flat.

"Oh, man!" I exclaimed and pulled over as quickly as I could, hoping I could stop before I ruined the tire. I was annoyed I'd have to unload most of my stuff out of the back to get at the spare, but not bothered by switching out tires. Usually, I kind of took it as a challenge to see how fast I could change the tire.

Jeff, his usual unfazed self, also got out of the car and headed to the flat tire.

He shook his head as we looked where chunks of tire were missing. "Looks like that tire's dead."

Still undaunted by the situation, I responded, "One nice thing with VW is they have a full-size spare."

We walked to the back and started pulling stuff out to clear off the back decking covering the spare. That took some work, but I finally pulled the tire out and bounced it on the ground, and as soon as I did it, I knew we were in trouble. Spare tires are supposed to bounce, not mush.

"Oh, man!" I exclaimed again, this time with much more feeling.

"It's flat," Jeff said, with a straight face.

"Thanks so much, I can see that."

"We passed an exit a couple miles back. Which tire do you want to take?"

I thought it over for a minute. There wasn't another way to do this that I could see. I guess some people call wreckers for things like this, but my inner penny-pincher wouldn't let me get away with it. Besides I didn't want to wait that long. "I guess let's take this one; it's not missing pieces. Maybe I won't have to buy a new tire and can get it aired up or have the hole fixed. I don't know why it'd be flat in the first place."

Jeff grabbed the tire. "I'll take the first shift of carrying it."

I didn't argue. I was busy kicking myself in the butt for going on a cross-country trip without checking to see if my spare was in good shape. What a stupid thing to do.

At a break in the traffic, we crossed our lanes, then the median, to the other side of the highway, in the hope someone would give us a ride, and started the walk back towards the exit, cars whizzing by.

Jeff looked at me. "Cheer up, friend. This isn't so bad." He smiled. "At least it's not--"

"No! Don't you dare say it!" I exclaimed. "Especially you! Don't you dare say it!"

Too late. Like every bad movie cliché, it started raining.

I looked over at him and glared, waiting to speak until after a particularly loud truck passed. "I didn't think a messiah would be such a jerk. This sucks. There's no way we can make it to Bethlehem tonight, so now I'll have to go to the new job exhausted from this trip. I'm sure I'll impress them going to my first-day half-dead."

At least it was summer and we were only getting wet, and not a cold, biting day, where we'd have to worry about hypothermia before we got to the exit.

Jeff shrugged. "This isn't that bad. It's all part of the experience."

"Yeah, right," I said back and ignored his chuckle.

As we walked, the phrase, "It's all part of the experience," echoed through my head, and I thought about the experiences like this in my life. From the perspective of hindsight, most of them weren't that big of a deal, but I couldn't say that for all experiences. This experience, however, was just inconvenient, that was all and not that big of a deal. On a normal trip, this might've been the most interesting thing that happened, and one of the best stories to tell. But on this trip, I doubted it'd even show up on my radar if I ever did tell anyone besides Beth about it.

I relaxed and figured I'd let this be what was happening and not get upset about it happening. "You want me to carry the tire now?"

He looked over at me with his expression that hadn't changed this whole time since the tire blew. He wasn't bothered in the least that we were walking down the highway in the rain carrying a flat tire. I'm not sure if he'd actually made it rain, either. It was cloudy before and... Crap! What'd it matter if he did or not? This is what's happening now, so I'd deal with it. It's all part of the experience.

"Sure, you can carry it. Let me know when you're tired and I'll take it back. If we take turns, it won't be that bad."

We fell silent for a while, until he said, "You know, once you've resigned yourself to the fact that you're going to get wet, walking in the rain is actually kind of nice. There's a certain peace to it. The highway ruins some of the effect, but if you can block that out, it's nice."

I looked at him but didn't reply. The rain ran down my face, it was a warm rain and the temperature was warm enough that the rain didn't make us cold. There was a peace to it.

We switched the tire back and forth a few more times before we finally made it to a gas station slash fast food place off the highway. We used the station's coin-operated air pump to fill the tire. With the recent rain, there were some nice deep puddles around, so Jeff and I took the tire to one and checked for an air leak. No bubbles appeared in the puddle, so apparently, it was low from dis-use, and our job was done. All we had to do now was to walk back to the car, change the tire, and get back on our way.

We started walking out of the parking lot, when a male voice called from behind us, "Hey, you guys look like you could use a ride."

Jeff and I turned and looked.

A young man, maybe eighteen years old, but most likely younger, was walking towards us. He briefly took notice of Jeff's battered face but said nothing.

Jeff said, "You don't need to do that, friend. We're soaked clear through, and I don't want to get your car all wet."

I looked at Jeff in horror. I'd resigned myself to walking back, but I sure wasn't going to turn down a ride.

The young man pointed at a very sorry looking car at the pump, then turned back to us with a smile. "I think you might be helping it out if you did."

Jeff smiled back. "Well, since you put it that way, then sure, a ride would be great."

I was vastly relieved to hear that, and we started towards his car, me carrying the tire.

"What's your name, friend?"

He said it was Derrick and we introduced ourselves.

Derrick said, "I need to finish filling up so you guys can drip dry for a little bit while I do that. Put the tire in the trunk."

As I put the tire in the trunk, I looked at Jeff. The guy who normally threw around money like it was nothing, didn't offer to buy gas for Derrick. And obviously, Derrick wasn't someone with an abundance of money, so I wondered what Jeff's reason was.

When Derrick got back from paying inside, I said, "Thanks for taking us back to the car. But it's a couple miles up, is that okay?"

"No problem, man. I know the feeling." He patted the top of his well-worn car. "The majority of the time, she gets me where I need to go, but when she doesn't, I've walked down the same highway as you. Not many times have people stopped to give this black kid a ride." He smiled.

His comment didn't strike me as if he was saying he was being discriminated against, his smile indicated humor instead of anger.

I was kind of interested in his angle so I responded with my own comment with my own smile, "Well, I know I've driven by my share of people, so I'm not that upset or surprised no one picked up these two white guys."

I was glad to see him enjoy the comment rather than take offense to it.

"You know that's true. I've driven by way too many people, too. I keep trying to reduce that number, and seeing you guys there was an easy call. I just got off work, it's on my way, and I've got time. Easy choice."

We all loaded into the car and headed out onto the highway.

Once at the Jetta, Derrick pulled up behind it and asked, "You guys got it okay, or you need help?"

I replied, "No, we got it under control."

Derrick smiled. "Okay. I'll leave you to it." But he didn't take off right away. After we had the car up on the jack, I guess he was comfortable we knew what we were doing, so he waved and drove off.

Jeff had a satisfied look on his face as he watched Derrick drive away.

As I loosened the lug nuts, I watched Jeff look at Derrick drive away. "Nothing for him? No book? No hundred-dollar bill?"

With a big smile, Jeff turned towards me. "Nope. He's on the path he needs to be on. At every fork in the road where he's had a choice, he's usually made the best one. The times he hasn't were used as times to learn. I'd have insulted him by offering money. He's of a rare class, nowadays. A person who won't take handouts and does what is right because it's right. Offering him money for helping us would've poisoned that in his mind."

Jeff glanced back down the highway, and then looked back down at me as I pulled the flat tire off. "Derrick's going to be just fine. He's having some tough times now, but he knows those are temporary. He knows it's all part of the experience."

I smiled at him and shook my head. This crazy man was starting to make so much sense. I knew exactly what he meant about Derrick.

* * *

We got our soggy selves back on the road, but it wasn't long before it was clear, walking in the rain and dealing with the tire had taken a lot more of my energy than I'd originally thought. We managed to make it to the Pennsylvania border before stopping for the night. That would leave about five hours of driving tomorrow.

Once I was settled into the hotel room, which Jeff paid for-- Derrick was a far better man than me because I was happy to take Jeff's handouts--I gave Beth a call.

She was surprised we weren't going to make it today. She knew how grueling this type of trip was and I would need some time to rest before work on Monday.

She then asked, "Did you get some answers?"

I thought about it for a second. "I did, in my mind at least. I asked him why a God of love would have a reward/punishment system like Heaven and Hell."

Beth had heard me complain about this type of thing repeatedly, "Okay, that question. I'll never understand why you just can't accept things."

This is why Beth and I don't talk about religion. She has no problem accepting things. They have to make sense to me, so our conversations rarely meet on any common ground.

Beth continued, "So, what was his answer?"

"He talked about some people in parts of today's world where everything needs to be explained in religious terms. 'God will reward you or God will punish you if you do X or Y.' He said that was the mentality of most people when Jesus was here. Saying pork carried bacteria that can make you sick if you don't cook it long enough wouldn't have worked."

"I guess I can see that."

"Now just listen, don't cut me off right away. Picture heaven as the fourth dimension, you have up/down and north/south, east/west, and some other direction we don't understand, because we are in three dimensions."

"Stanley!"

I know how this sounded to her. It was more Stanley-crazy-talk. "Just listen. So spatially, Heaven is very complex. Emotionally it's even more complex. Jeff says all of your emotions are amplified. So, if you're a person whose heart is filled with love, and you die and go to the next dimension where your love is amplified so you are..." I left it open hoping Beth would understand.

She paused for a brief moment. "You'd be in Heaven?"

"Right! And if hate and anger were what filled your heart here?"

"You'd be in Hell?" she answered.

"Exactly! And it's not a judgment that condemns you or rewards you. It's you doing it to yourself."

Her voice let me know she wasn't convinced, "It's creative; I'll give you that. If it starts bringing you closer to Christianity, gets you looking at it seriously, then I'm all for it."

"Imagine how that would have sounded to the people Jesus was talking to," I added.

"It makes sense Jesus would have talked to the people of that time at a level they would understand, but I don't know if your explanation makes any sense. And besides, wouldn't that basically make Heaven on Earth also. I mean, if you are living with love driving your life now, wouldn't that make your life much better? And the more people who do it, the closer we are to the Kingdom of God here on Earth?"

As she said that I had an image of Jeff watching Derrick drive away. I'd never seen Jeff watch someone in wonder like that. Even if I wasn't with Jeff, Derrick would've stood out to me. From the moment he walked up to us, there was something different about him, and after he started talking, there was a calmness and depth to his words. "Beth, I think you're brilliant. I think you are exactly right." That Derrick, with his heart full of love, was very close to Heaven here on Earth.

We talked for a bit more, and then I talked to the kids for a while. As with every time I get off the phone with them, I dreaded the coming two months. I hung up the phone feeling a little down.

\* \* \*

I woke up Sunday morning wondering how I was going to make it through work Monday. My original plan had been to give myself two days to recover from the trip, but the reality was I was going to get into Bethlehem with just a half of a day to recover.

But how could I complain? This wasn't merely the experience of a lifetime; it was the experience of a millennium or two. And as Jeff liked to say, it's all part of the experience.

Even if I was tired, I'd be able to get through my first day of work. It just may not be pleasant.

I took my shower, and as I picked up the hair conditioner, I was thankful Jeff and I wouldn't have to kill anyone from the room service staff. I laughed to myself and imagined the rest of my life would be spent reflecting on this week.

So far, it'd been overwhelming and what it all meant was incomprehensible.

I guess if I'd have imagined myself on a trip with the messiah, or whatever Jeff actually was, I'd have thought I'd be asking for all of the answers to all of those questions that had filled my mind my whole life. But that wasn't how this trip had worked so far.

True, I'd had a couple critical questions answered, but the rest of the time had been the experiences and the conversation. And even the questions I did ask seemed to fit more in Jeff's timing than with mine.

As I dressed, I tried to make a plan for the rest of the time with Jeff. Should I ask more questions and if so, what questions? But the more I played with the idea, the more it seemed like I should let the day be the day it turned out to be. As I reached that conclusion, there was a knock on the door. I couldn't help but think the timing was not by chance. Nothing on this trip had been by chance, no matter how much it seemed like it. I was sure Jeff was giving me the time to come to the conclusion I had come to before he came to my room.

"Come in!" I called out.

The man with no key to my room opened the door and walked in. He wore his usual smile. His face was looking a little better, the swelling was going down some and the bruising was turning a gruesome shade of greenish-yellow. "Did you sleep good, friend?"

I thought about it for a second. "You know, actually, I did sleep pretty good. And you?"

Looking at him as I said it, I wondered how could someone as bruised and beaten up as he was radiate with happiness like he did?

"About the same as normal," he answered.

After finishing getting ready, I grabbed my stuff and threw it in the Jetta as we walked by on the way to a nearby restaurant for breakfast. The Jetta was in a different parking spot than we parked it last night, so I assumed Jeff had filled it. Obviously, Jeff didn't like to ride in a car if he didn't have to, so we walked the two blocks to the restaurant. I didn't mind. It was in the low seventies and a beautiful morning. Thankfully, we had breakfast without any events happening.

We walked back, got in the car, and started down the road. With all the green trees and rolling hills, it was an alluring drive.

We drove more while all of this was setting in. Maybe I should've let Jeff drive because my mind was nowhere near the car, the road or the traffic. I was deep in my own head undoing and redoing synaptic pathways. Somehow, I didn't crash, and I looked up to see we were pulling up to the city limits of Bethlehem.

We'd missed lunch and I hadn't even realized it.

I looked over at Jeff, who he was in his normal state when we weren't talking, reading a book.

I started to panic. Somehow, I'd wasted my last five hours with Jeff, totally absorbed in my own thoughts. All the questions I should've asked started flooding my mind, but it was too late. I'd blown it.

I regained my composure and asked, "Where do you want me to drop you off?" And as I asked it, I wondered how I really felt about it. I'd been on the strangest cross-country trip one could ever imagine. Now the trip was over, I hadn't come close to taking advantage of it, and now I'd have to spend a lifetime making sense of what happened and kicking myself in the butt for not taking advantage of the time I had with him.

He responded, "You can drop me off pretty much anywhere in town. I can make it from there."

"I can take you wherever you need to go. I have some time." All I had planned for the rest of the day was kicking myself in the butt.

"No need for that. I've been crammed in a car for long enough. I'd like to walk for a while."

We pulled into town and he pointed to a parking lot for me to pull into. Jeff leaned over and hugged me, whether I wanted it or not, and said, "I love you, friend. I can't thank you enough for the ride." With that, he started to get out, but I stopped him.

"Now what?" I asked a little desperately.

He smiled at me. "Same as always, Stanley. Live your life."

"But I have so many more questions. I didn't ask you all I should've asked you. I--"

Jeff stopped me. "No, that isn't true. You asked me the

questions you needed answered. You'll always have more questions and that's a beautiful thing. Look for answers and you'll find them. You don't need me to answer them, and if you feel you do, I'll always be with you. God, Jesus, and I never left you, Stanley, and in the same way, our time is not up either." He looked at me deeply. "You got from this trip what you needed from this trip. Now, use it to get more out of the rest of your trip."

I looked out the front window as I thought about what he said, about my time not being up with him in the same way as God and Jesus, and then turned my focus back to Jeff. It wasn't the same. This was it. My time with him was up. "I love you, too."

He could tell I was not taking this well. "I *will* always be with you, friend. When you have questions, they will be answered. They may not be answered in a detailed point by point written format, but if you keep your eyes open, they will be answered. All you need to do is keep moving forward and asking questions. The core of your being is where it needs to be, so even if you take wrong turns with your choices, in the end, you will always end up moving in the right direction. The biggest thing for you to remember is wrong turns are part of the path, not a distraction from the path."

Hearing him say that calmed my nerves some. It gave me some faith in myself, and faith in any form isn't something I've ever been good at.

Jeff got out of the car, shut the door, and walked away.

Stanley's story continues in:
**"The Infinite Jeff – Part 2"**

# Book List

One thing I repeatedly get asked for is a list of books mentioned in *The Infinite Jeff*. Jeff sees reading as one of the greatest activities to promote vertical growth. I couldn't agree more.

*Walden* – Henry David Thoreau

*If I ran the Zoo* – Dr. Seuss

*Illusions* – Richard Bach

*A Tree Grows in Brooklyn* – Betty Smith

*Stranger in a Strange Land* – Robert A. Heinlein

*Jubal Sackett* – Louis L'Amour

*Twelve Steps to a Compassionate Life* – Karen Armstrong

*Beyond Good and Evil* – Friedrich Nietzsche

*Flatland: A Romance of Many Dimensions* – Edwin Abbott Abbott

*Man's Search for Meaning* – Viktor E. Frankl

*Sadhana: The Realization of Life* – Rabindranath Tagore

*Stealing Jesus* – Bruce Bawer

*Green Eggs and Ham* – Dr. Seuss

*The Language of God* – Francis S. Collins

*The Divine Comedy* – Dante Alighieri

Made in the USA
Monee, IL
11 March 2022

92738457R00105